THE SHIFTING CURRENT

A COASTAL GUARDIANS NOVELLA

DANI PETTREY

BOOKS BY DANI PETTREY

Copyright © 2022 by Dani Marlene Pettrey

Cover Design © James T. Egan of Bookfly Design

Author Photograph by Mike Pettrey of MVP Photography

Author is represented by Janet Grant of Books & Such Literary Management

ISBN: 979-8218021306

Series: Coastal Guardians ; sequel novella

For my husband

Writing this book reminded me of our cowboy years in New Mexico. Of our fun road trips to nowhere in particular, horseback riding, and especially the day we met. I can still see you waltzing up to me in your black, felt Stetson asking me to dance.

It's turned out to be the dance of a lifetime. I love you beyond measure.

PROLOGUE

Death. It permeated her hair, her skin. She wanted to crawl out of it, but there was nowhere to go.

Jeff depressed the accelerator to the floorboard, putting distance between her and the body. But more was required. Infinitely more.

She feared she'd never outrun it.

The booming ricochet of the shotgun still rang in her ears.

Stop! She scratched at them. Why wouldn't it stop?

Cold slithered down her face.

"You're clammy." He chucked a rag at her, but it reeked of blood.

Her stomach churned. She pressed the back of her hand against her mouth.

"You aren't going to hurl, are you? Amateur."

He flew over the hill.

"Slow down," she eked out. "You'll get us pulled over."

"Yeah." He chuckled. "If you get arrested, he'll know you didn't follow the plan. Then you'll be as good as dead."

She already was. It was just a matter of time before he figured it out and came for her.

ONE

Special Agent Logan Perry, of the Coast Guard Investigative Service, passed his teammate Emmalyne Thorton's yellow Mini Cooper in the station lot. Warmth filled him despite the record low temperatures in Wilmington this winter. He loved his job. Thrived at it. But of late, he came for her. For Em.

Opening the station door, heat wafted out. He pulled the door shut tight behind him and turned to find his boss headed straight toward him.

"Hey, Noah. You heading out?"

"Hey, Logan. Nope, just grabbing a file I left in the Jeep." He glanced at his watch. "Only fifteen minutes early for shift." He grinned. "Losing your touch, man?"

Logan grinned back. "My touch is just fine."

Noah chuckled. Frigid wind whisked in as his boss stepped out.

Slipping out of his coat, Logan glanced at Em's desk only to find it empty.

"Hey, Logan," his teammate Rissi greeted him.

"Hey, Ris. Working late?" He glanced at the clock. Her shift had ended hours ago.

"Nah. I told Em I'd cover her shift."

"Oh." His shoulders slumped of their own accord even as his curiosity surged. Em always made her shifts—*their* shift. Due to the compatibility of their combined skillsets, Noah partnered them together on the vast majority of cases. Together, they were nearly unstoppable at tracking down leads. On a personal level... He knew he didn't have the right to ask for anything there, no matter how much he wanted to. But he relished every minute he got to spend with her, even if they couldn't be anything more than coworkers and friends. "She say why she needed you to cover her shift?" he couldn't help but ask.

"She had a date."

Date? He swallowed. "Did she say with who?"

"Nope," Rissi said, flipping through a file on her desk. "I was in the lab with Finn when she left earlier, but I caught a glimpse of her in the hallway. She looked drop-dead gorgeous."

"Oh...she left from here?"

"Yep. Said she'd be back for her car after." A knowing smirk crossed Rissi's face.

Was he that obvious?

He cleared his throat. "Time to get to work." He settled in his desk, logged into his laptop, and tried to throw himself fully into wrapping up the paperwork from their last case, but it was nigh impossible. Em tracked through his mind.

He glanced at the clock. 2100. Two hours and still no Emmy. Anxiety gnawed at the pit of his stomach. He had to release some restless energy. He stood and stretched. "I think I'll get some fresh air." He yanked his coat off the back of his chair and headed for the door.

Stepping outside, wind slapped his cheeks, his breath

clouding in the crisp night air. Frost blanketed the crunchy grass, and the exterior light illuminated a layer of snow and patches of ice across the parking lot. Thick flakes fell about his shoulders.

Winter sea swells—perfect for surfing—were common. Snow was not. It was the first snowfall he'd experienced since he'd moved to Wilmington years ago. On any other day, that detail might have held his interest. But today? Not so much.

He looked at his watch. 2115. How much longer could a dinner date last? And who was Emmy with? He was being ridiculous, and he knew it. He had no claim on Em. It was perfectly reasonable for her to date and to stay out with her date for as long as she pleased. He had no say in the matter, despite how deeply his heart ached for her.

After a handful of moments, he headed back inside to his paperwork.

Twenty grueling minutes later, the station door opened, and Emmy entered.

Logan stared, slack-jawed, at the vision before him. His eyes widened. *Em?*

Not that she wasn't always beautiful, but tonight...her hair was elegantly arranged, with wispy tendrils caressing her neck; emerald earrings dangled from her ears, contrasting beautifully against her fair skin; light makeup highlighted her vibrant eyes and made them glow.

He was so caught up in the sight of her that it took a second to notice she was followed by Major Burton James, in full Marine dress blues.

"Burton?" Logan managed to mutter despite the shock roiling through him. He took in the man's dress blues. "A Marine Corps Ball?" he asked.

"Yes," Burton clipped—always straight to the point. He

took off his Corps-issued white hat, holding it in his equally white dress gloves. "Our command post dance."

Logan's gaze flicked back to Emmy, who had taken off her coat. She looked enchanting. Her dress was the color of the water surrounding the east Indonesian island of Morotai. He had thought the jade and azure waters he'd viewed during his island escape would always be the most breathtaking thing he'd ever seen, but he'd been wrong. Emmy left them in the dust.

She turned to Burton, stepping in front of him before he could proceed any further into the station. "I had a nice time tonight. Thank you for the invite."

Burton dipped his head and lifted her hand to his lips, pressing a kiss to it. "Thank you for the pleasure of your company," he said, slipping his hat back on. He swiped his hand across the black brim—the gold Marine Corps insignia in the center of the white.

She smiled. "No, thank *you*."

"Good evening." Burton nodded once at the group, then turned on the heel of his meticulously shined black dress shoes. He stepped out the door, snowflakes fluttering around him.

As soon as the door shut, Logan turned to Emmy. "Burton James? *Really*, Em?"

Noah cleared his throat. "I'm going to grab a cup of coffee. It's going to be a long night. Rissi, you want to join me for a cup?"

"Yep." Rissi sprang from her chair and trailed Noah into the kitchen.

"What's wrong with Burton?" Emmy asked, frowning as she hung up her coat before turning back to him, hands on her hips. Logan's mouth went dry. The silky material of her dress hugged her curves perfectly.

"He's a player." One that rivaled Logan's own player days.

She exhaled. "So many adages...which to choose? Maybe...

'pot, kettle.' Or 'don't throw stones.' Or maybe just 'it takes one to know one.'"

That barb stung deeper than he'd anticipated. That was what she thought of him—*still*. That he was a player on par with Burton James. Even on his worst days, he'd always had far more respect for women than Burton.

He closed his eyes, absorbing the pain, then opened them on an exhale.

Please, Father, I know she would never choose me, but don't let her choose someone so unworthy of her. Not a man like Burton James.

His cell phone rang, yanking him from his prayer. Clearing his throat, he answered on the second ring. "Perry," he said.

"Logan, it's Tom."

"Hey, Tom. It's been a while." At least a month since his high-school-buddy-turned-hometown-sheriff had called to chat through a case.

"I'm afraid this isn't a catch-up call," Tom said, his tone uneasy, stilted.

"What's up?" he asked slowly, not liking the tension in his friend's voice.

"It's Colt. Something...something's happened."

His grandfather? Logan shook his head, bewildered. What could have happened? They'd talked just the other day. "Is he hurt?" The old man was the picture of health, but that didn't stop accidents from happening. Had there been a car crash? A fall?

Tom released a whoosh of air. "Man..." he said, a catch in his throat. "I don't know how else to say this other than to shoot straight."

Logan frowned. "How bad is it? Is he in the hospital?"

"No, I'm afraid it's too late for that. Logan, your grandfather's been murdered."

TWO

Logan's cell slipped from his hand, careening to the floor. "Logan?" Em hurried to his side, retrieving his phone and handing it back to him. "What's wrong? You just went pale."

His throat squeezed, but he managed to choke out, "My grandpa's been murdered."

A gasp escaped Em's lips. "Oh, Logan, I'm so sorry," she said. Rissi and Noah, now back in the main station bay, added their condolences.

Logan lifted the phone back to his ear. "I'll be on the next plane out," Logan said to Tom, darting a glance at Noah, who nodded.

"I figured. I'll see you when you get here," Tom said. "Send your flight info, so I know when to expect you."

"Will do." Logan hung up, his brain in a haze.

"I'll book your ticket," Rissi said. "Just give me your login details."

Logan scribbled them down.

"*Our* tickets," Em said.

"Em, you don't—" Logan began.

Emmy held up a hand, cutting him off. "Don't bother," she said, her tone as resolute as her firm, upheld hand. "I've made up my mind, and we both know I won't be changing it." She looked to Noah. "Of course, if that's okay with you, sir?"

"Please," Noah said, "you both go. Take as long as you need. Just keep us updated, and let us know if we can be of help in any way."

"Thanks, boss," Em said.

"Of course." Noah turned to Rissi. "See if you can get them on the next plane out, even if it means we have to ride to the airport with sirens on."

"On it," she said, turning to her computer.

"Em, you can't go without anything," Logan said. "I have stuff there for when I visit, but you'll need some clothes and—"

"I'm good," she said. "Just need five." She hurried to the women's locker room.

A handful of moments later, she emerged wearing a black maxi skirt and a jade silk blouse—probably what she'd been wearing earlier before she'd changed for the ball. She also held up a duffle. "I always keep a few things here just in case."

"Okay," Rissi said, spinning around in her chair. "You're on the last flight out." She looked at the clock on the wall. "You'd best hurry."

An hour and a half later, they were aboard the first leg of their flight to Silver City, New Mexico.

He glanced over at Em settling into her seat, stashing a book she'd snagged from her desk in the seatback pocket in front of her. He was so grateful she'd come. He couldn't explain it, but her presence always brought an inexplicable peace to his soul. But tonight, that peace warred with anguish from the devastation of losing Colt in four words. *"Your grandfather's been murdered."* The stark reality of how finite time was lodged

9

in Logan's throat. He shifted his gaze forward as tears burned his eyes. He couldn't break down in front of Em. He needed to be strong for her...for Colt.

The flight attendant handed them heated towels as they prepared for takeoff.

He wiped his face, surprised he could feel the warmth. He'd been numb since Tom's call. He handed it back to the attendant, thanked her, and shifted his attention back on Em.

She reached over and placed her delicate hand atop his on the armrest separating them.

"We'll get whoever did this. You know that, right?" she said.

He prayed with everything in him that that was true.

"Logan?" Em gave his hand a gentle shake. "You *know* that, right?"

He looked over at her, entwining his fingers with hers. "Together, there's nothing we can't do." He believed that with his whole heart, to a far greater degree than she realized. He ached to wrap her in his arms...to hold her tight...to find comfort in her embrace—now more than ever. But he had no right to any of that.

The engines roared and they taxied down the runway before soaring up in the sky, the pressure pushing Logan against his seat.

He looked to Em. "You'd best get some rest. We've got an hour and a half before our layover in Atlanta."

She nodded, her eyes fluttering closed before too long.

She looked so peaceful in sleep.

Slipping his hand into his leather knapsack, he pulled out his book and booklight. No way he'd find sleep tonight.

He flipped to the spot where he'd left off in Jeffery Deaver's latest novel and clipped his booklight in place. He needed something...*anything*...to distract him until he could arrive home and finally be useful. He took a sharp inhale, still struggling to understand who would kill Colt.

While he'd been deemed a crotchety, gruff man by the old biddies in town, Logan's grandpa possessed the heart of a cowboy poet. No one so gentle and good with horses...with any animal...could truly be crotchety. The women just didn't like his lack of conversation. Colt only spoke when there was something worth saying—and then, he was filter-free, always speaking the unvarnished truth, though without ever being judgmental or unkind. Or at least, he always had. Past tense. His grandfather—the man who had taken him in and raised him after Logan's father had dumped him on Colt's doorstep—now existed in the past tense.

Logan forced his attention back to the words on the page. *Focus.* But it was no use. His fifth time through the first sentence, he gave up.

Thoughts of the last time he'd seen Colt streamed through his mind. October. Good memories of the visit flooded his mind, but...Christmas. He hadn't gone home for the first time. His chest squeezed. If he'd gone, maybe...

Why hadn't he gone? He exhaled. He knew exactly why. She was asleep beside him. Once he'd learned she'd be staying in town for the holidays, he hadn't been able to resist staying with her. Seeing her face when she'd opened the gift from him had been priceless. But he could have flown home—what had been *his home* since he was five—the following day. Instead, he'd waited, assuming there'd be plenty of time to see Colt later. But now, time was gone.

THREE

Logan rested his hand on Em's lower back, directing her through the small airport, heading outside for the rental car building at the far end of the parking lot. His steady gait hitched at the sight of the exit doors.

"You all right?" Em asked.

He nodded, feeling anything but.

Every time he'd stepped out those doors, Colt had been waiting on the other side. But not today. Not ever again.

His chest tightened as they exited the terminal, stepping out into the cold night air lingering, sunrise still a half hour away.

His gaze anchored on the chain-link fence Colt always used to lean against, his gray felt Stetson tipped back, a wad of sunflower seeds perpetually in his right cheek ever since Mee-Maw had gotten him to stop dipping. As soon as Colt caught sight of him, he'd practically spring off the fence, welcoming him with a broad smile on his weathered face and a twinkle in his old, crinkly blue eyes.

Logan swallowed and pinched the bridge of his nose. He didn't want to think of a world without Colt in it.

The man was a legend in more ways than one—larger than life to a young, scared boy. Larger than life to a lost, twenty-eight-year-old man.

"Logan," a deep, familiar voice said.

He turned to find Tom Mahoney, dressed in the tan shirt and brown pants of a sheriff's uniform, leaning against one of the parking lot's light poles—the glow from the lights muting the cluster of stars overhead.

Tom swiped off his straw hat and clutched it between hands still calloused from his rodeo days. He cleared his throat and stepped up to meet them. "I can't begin to tell you how sorry I am." He fidgeted with the brim of his hat. "You've got to know that was the last call I ever wanted to make."

Logan squeezed his friend's shoulder. "I know, man." Tom was basically an adopted grandson to Colt—when they were kids, he'd spent more time on their ranch than at his family's house in town.

Tom's gaze shifted over Logan's shoulder to rest on Emmy.

"Sorry," Logan said. "I forgot my manners. "Tom, this is Emmy, my..." *Friend? Love of my life?* "...my colleague."

Em's jaw tightened.

He frowned. Had she wanted him to give her a title of deeper significance? *No.* His head was a mess. He wasn't thinking straight. "Sorry," Logan continued. "What I should have said is, this is CGIS Special Agent Emmalyne Thorton. Em, this is Cauldron County Sherriff Tom Mahoney."

"Agent Thorton." Tom nodded.

"Emmy, please," she said, shaking Tom's outstretched hand. "Nice to meet you, Sheriff."

"Tom, please, ma'am."

"Tom it is." She smiled.

"I've got the patrol vehicle over here." Tom gestured to a white and blue Tahoe labeled *Sheriff* in the drop-off zone, and they followed him towards it.

"You didn't have to come all this way." Cauldron Creek was an hour-and-a-half drive from the airport.

"I didn't want you bothering with some rental."

"Thanks. I appreciate the ride. This way, I can just use Colt's pickup in town."

Tom paused a few feet from the SUV.

"What is it?" Logan asked, his shoulders tensing. Whatever his friend was holding back was nothing good, judging by the jagged crease on Tom's brow.

Tom slid his index fingers through his belt loop and rocked back on the heels of his tan Ropers, stalling the same way he had ever since they were kids.

"Tom?" he pressed as Em stepped up beside him, her freesia perfume wafting floral scents amid the swift winds howling through the terminal lot.

Tom rubbed the back of his neck, then shook his head on a solemn whistle. "Again, I hate to tell you this, but it's either me or Deputy Winston."

"Denton?" Logan blinked. "*He's* still your deputy?"

"Denton may be obnoxious, but he does fine police work."

"Okay..." He put aside thoughts of that topic—or rather, that person—for the moment. "What is it?"

Tom sighed...and then finally let it out. "She stole Colt's truck."

Logan blinked. "I'm sorry...did you just say *she?*" There had to be a mistake. Colt hadn't so much as looked at another woman since Mee-Maw passed over a decade ago.

"Your grandpa let a drifter woman stay in one of the bunkhouses. Went by Mary, but who knows if that's her real name."

Despite his salty demeanor with townsfolk—primarily with the town biddies—Colt always was too trusting. "Is she the one who murdered him?" Someone who Colt had taken in out of the goodness of his heart had betrayed him in such an awful, ruthless way? Heat rushed through Logan's veins, anger bubbling inside.

"She's our top suspect."

"Please tell me she's in custody."

Tom swallowed, his Adam's apple bobbing. "Afraid not. Living out of town on the ranch...it wasn't like a neighbor was going to call in the shots—" Tom stopped short. "Sorry. Didn't mean to just blurt out the details like that. It's just...you and I typically talk cases from the investigator's perspective, not..."

"Not as the victim's family." Logan released a pent-up breath. "I get it. No need to apologize. I'd rather you treat me like another investigator. Because I am."

"One who is far too close to this case."

"Please don't make me sit this one out." He didn't have it in him. "We can help."

"That's what your boss"—Tom indicated both Logan and Emmy—"said for over an hour."

The tiniest hint of a smile formed on Logan's lips. Noah had gone to bat for them.

"He started by suggesting that it would be a professional courtesy to make you an official part of the investigation, and when I hesitated, he proceeded to go through all the ways you and Emmy, here, could be of assistance, given your specific skill sets."

"And?"

"It's impressive."

"And?" Logan pushed.

Please, Lord, don't make me sit this one out. I need to help. Need to do something.

Tom exhaled. "I'll share what I deem prudent, but you also understand Denton is my deputy. He'll be working this case too."

Logan tilted his head back, staring at the sky as he silently prayed for strength. Working a case with Denton Winston. That'd be a first, and something he was far from looking forward to. Finally, he let his head drop, meeting Tom's gaze. "Well, we won't make any progress standing around here. Let's get to town."

Tom unlocked the patrol vehicle with the keypad, the lights flashing in sync with a loud beeping. "Hop on in," Tom said. "We've got a solid ride back."

"All right," Logan said, opening the front passenger door for Em, but she moved for the back seat.

He cocked his head. "Em?"

"I'm good back here. I can stretch my legs out while you two talk."

As soon as they hit the highway, Logan shifted to face Tom and rested his back against the locked passenger door. "So, I'm going to have to work with Denton some?"

"That's right," Tom agreed, sounding apologetic.

Em leaned forward, studying Logan's expression. "I've gotta ask, what's the deal with this guy?"

"You know the obnoxious jock guy who just never grew up?" Logan said.

"Yeah."

He dipped his chin and arched his brows.

"Gotcha. But surely after all these years and with the loss... with what happened..."

"We'll work this out one way or another," Tom said.

"Thanks, Tom."

"But that doesn't mean you have free rein, either." Tom glanced over at him. "You got me?"

Logan nodded. "I got you."

"Now that's settled," Tom said, "I'll share the basics."

"The woman. How much of a head start does she have?" Logan rattled off the first of the questions racing through his mind.

"The FDMI—" Tom paused and glanced at Emmy in the rearview mirror. "Here we have a Field Deputy Medical Investigator come out from Albuquerque to work the crime scene," he said. "I know it's a mouthful."

"Nah, I got it," Emmy said. "Thanks for explaining."

He gave Logan a quick sideways glance before directing his gaze fully back on the road. "The field investigator placed time of death shortly between six and six-thirty p.m. local time."

"And the—" Logan curled his fingers into a fist. Colt wasn't a victim or a body. He was his grandpa. "And Colt was found at what time?"

"Bucky went to take him some of Caroline's homemade biscochitos around half past seven. You know how she likes... liked...to dote on him."

Logan glanced back at Em. "Bucky's the ranch hand."

She nodded. "Thanks."

He turned his attention back to Tom. "Once Bucky called it in, how long did it take you guys to arrive and then determine that the woman and Colt's truck were both gone?"

"Probably a half hour."

Logan's fist tightened. "So she had a minimum hour-and-a-half-head start before Denton started looking for her."

"Yeah." Tom rubbed the back of his neck. "That's what we're working with. We had barricades up for a handful of hours after..." Tom cleared his throat. "BoBorder Patrol is on alert, and there's a BOLO on the truck."

"And her..." Logan said. "You have her picture plastered all over the news? We both know she probably dumped Colt's truck as soon as possible."

"Uh..." Tom swallowed, hunching his shoulders. "We're working on that."

Logan narrowed his eyes. "Meaning?"

"Other than Colt—and Denton, when he caught her off guard once..." Tom released a shaky exhale. "—no one else got a decent look at her face. Not even Bucky."

"What? How is that possible?"

"The woman kept to herself. When she did venture out of the bunkhouse, according to Bucky, she always wore a gray hoodie with the hood up. He said it shadowed most of her face. She never made eye contact, kept her head down. Never went into town."

"Didn't Colt or Bucky—or Denton, especially—find that odd?"

"Colt assumed she was running from someone."

"Like the law?" Em asked.

"Nah. He figured it was an abusive ex. I think that's why he was so kind to her. Let her bunk up, fed her, loaned her the pickup a couple times."

Em's nose scrunched. "If she borrowed the truck but didn't go into town, then where did she go?"

"That's question number four on our list."

"What are numbers one through three?" Em asked before Logan could.

Tom glanced back, his left arm draped over the wheel, before shooting Logan a sideways smile. "You've got a good partner here," he said.

Logan looked to Em and nodded. "Yes, I do." If only she was more than his work partner. Life partner was what he ached for, even if he knew it wasn't possible. Not with the baggage he carried from his past.

"Thanks," she said. "So...numbers one through three?"

"Number one: Where she is now? Number two: What does she look like? We're waiting for a sketch artist to come in from Albuquerque so Denton can describe her. The field investigator said he'd send one out as soon as one's available, but who knows how long that will be? But getting a clear image of her should help us get a match on her full identity—name, last known address, prior arrest record if she has one...and I'm thinking she probably does. Number three: What did she do with the items she stole? If we can find them, that will hopefully give us a lead on number one—discovering at least the direction she's heading."

"Gotcha," Em said. "But there's no need to wait on a sketch artist."

Tom glanced in the rearview mirror at her. "No?"

"Nope. Logan's our team's sketch artist," she said.

"Really?" Tom said, a furrow of surprise on his brow.

"Yes." Logan nodded. But draw the woman who'd killed Colt? Look into a charcoal rendition of her eyes while he sketched each line, thumbed the strokes of shading... It would be gut-wrenching.

But he'd do it. Anything to hunt down Colt's killer.

FOUR

"I didn't know you still sketched," Tom said, glancing over at Logan.

Still? Emmy crossed her legs. Intriguing. She'd seen his skills as a sketch artist, but she'd never heard him talking about doing any drawing outside of the job. Tom made it sound like it was a longstanding hobby. She'd love to see the sketches he'd done outside of work, if he'd kept any of them.

"All right, then." Tom tapped the wheel. "We'll head to the station and then on to the ranch."

Logan nodded. "Can we shift to question number three?" he asked.

"Sure," Tom said.

"What did she take?" Logan asked.

"That's where you come in," Tom said. "When you're up to it, we'll need you to walk through the house and see what's been taken."

"You believe she stole more than the truck?" Logan asked.

Tom nodded. "At least one other item is gone."

Logan's shoulders tensed.

"What?" Em asked, her gaze bouncing between the two of them. What was she missing?

"Colt's gun," Logan said.

"Oh. I'm sorry." She bit her bottom lip. The fear someone would use the gun to harm someone else always hung heavy with the owner. "I'm sure we'll find it," she said. They knew how to track things down—some...*many* that were considered untraceable by those around them.

Tom glanced over to Logan, and Em caught his nod.

She narrowed her eyes. "What aren't you saying?"

"Colt was my grandpa's nickname, not his given name," Logan said.

"Okay, so I'm guessing he owned a Colt?" Must have been a pretty nice one if everyone considered it such a big deal that they'd nickname the man after it.

"Not just any Colt," Tom said. "An 1873 Colt .45 Peace-maker—originally owned by Colt's great-great-grandaddy, U.S. Marshal Brady Tucker."

"Oh," Em said, crossing one leg over the other, smoothing her maxi skirt across her lap. That was some gun. "Just out of curiosity, what was his given name?"

Tom arched his brows at Logan in the rearview mirror.

"Logan Brady Tucker," he said.

"You're named after him?"

"Yeah." Logan's voice cracked.

"We'll get the gun back," she said, certain of that fact. There wasn't anything they couldn't hunt down—and based on the drifter suspect, it was very likely the lady had pawned it. Though "lady" wasn't a term a murderess deserved.

Logan nodded.

She wanted to reassure him more. Say, "we've got this," but she didn't want to disrespect Tom or imply that his team wasn't capable of handling the investigation. But no way would Logan sit on the sidelines. He didn't have it in him. And whatever he needed from her, she'd be right there. They were partners.

Partners. She sniffed back the emotions banging at her ribcage. He'd called her a colleague earlier. She'd hoped for more. How much more didn't matter. The one barrier she'd believed eliminated any chance of them being "more" was his lack of faith. Since he'd asked Christ to be his Savior, that barrier was gone. The one that existed between them now was a far more personal one. But this certainly wasn't the time to be thinking about that.

Tom tapped the steering wheel. "There is one area we need to come to terms on if I'm bringing you in on this."

"Which is?" Logan asked.

"You have to remember to wait for my lead and..."

Em managed to contain a small chuckle. It was no time to laugh, but Logan looked like a jack-in-the-box toy, ready to spring on whatever area of access Tom gave them.

"And you need to respect Denton as my deputy," he said.

Logan released a pent-up exhale.

"I know that ain't going to be easy, but he's actually a good officer—and what went down between you two happened a long time ago," Tom said.

Logan sat back. "I doubt Denton views it that way."

M ary paced the small cell...okay, it was a motel room, but it felt like a prison cell—and the thought of being in a real one terrified her. What had she done?

Biting the nib of her nail bed, the rest of the nail gone from her nasty habit, she continued cutting a swath across the orange shag carpet. Jeff really knew how to pick 'em. But his argument that no one would find her here seemed sound, at least on the surface.

The truck was stashed at a truck stop, less than a mile's walk away. He'd wedged it behind the row of semis, far in the back near the dumpster. Even if it was found before he returned, it wouldn't lead to where she was. Not directly. Or so she hoped, anyway. Her head was a mess. What sounded right could be fully upside-down for all she knew.

Biting her bottom lip, her heart thwacking in her chest, she toyed with the notion of jumping in the truck and taking off, leaving the Southwest in her rearview mirror, but Jeff was right. He'd find her.

She'd deviated from the plan. For whatever reason, Jeff was helping her, keeping her off his radar. Maybe he cared about her after all...but that didn't seem right. She'd learned a long time ago to never be dependent on anyone, and yet her addiction made dependence a way of life. She'd already paid for it in more ways than one. But this time, she was fully in over her head, drowning in the suffocating depths with no way out. As much as she tried to convince herself otherwise, she knew the truth. He'd figure out she'd deviated from the plan. He'd find her and he'd kill her—in a far more brutal way than the old man.

FIVE

T om waved at a woman waiting at the crosswalk.

Em had been so focused on the discussion and Logan's reactions that she hadn't even realized they'd entered town.

A line of storefronts ran along either side of the paved two-lane road for a handful of blocks, then simply ended at the side of a terra-cotta-colored cliff. Layers of strata in deepening hues ran up the wall until it morphed into a stand of...junipers, maybe? Along with another tree she was familiar with but couldn't name.

The woman waved back at Tom upon reaching the other side of the street, joining the group of ladies awaiting her. Soon, they were all waving.

Tom rolled the window down. "Morning, ladies."

"That dang rattler nearly took Bo's front paw off this morning," an elderly woman vented as the gathering women bustled up in front of a quaint diner. Em looked up at the sign. *Melvin's Place.*

"I'm sorry to hear that, Ms. Baca," Tom said. "Gotta keep

an eye out for them under cars."

Em widened her eyes, and a soft smile creased Logan's pained expression.

"It's okay. I've got you," he whispered, keeping his back shifted towards the ladies.

She smiled, then narrowed her eyes. Was he purposely keeping his back to the women?

"Now how is that going to help with Bo's vet bill?" Ms. Baca propped her hand on her robust hip.

"I'm sorry, ma'am, but the sheriff's department can't be in charge of rattlers." Tom's tone was polite, but the phrase felt worn with repetition.

Em would bet this wasn't the first time he'd had this conversation with the woman.

"When—" Ms. Baca started, then stopped short. She narrowed her eyes, spiderweb creases fanning out along her pale skin. She stepped toward the vehicle, which reminded Em they were still sitting at the crosswalk.

Em turned. Not a single car behind them. She turned back around as Ms. Baca approached the passenger window.

"Is that you, Logan?" she asked.

With a deep sigh and a quick pinch to the bridge of his nose, Logan shifted around to face Ms. Baca.

She smiled. "It *is* you, and even more handsome than the last time I saw you." Ms. Baca squeezed his cheeks.

Em bit her lip, trying not to laugh as Logan scrunched his face. If this had been any other visit, any other circumstances, this would have served her as fodder for teasing for months. But in *these* circumstances, laughing—no matter the reason—felt innately wrong.

"Nice to see you, Ms. Baca," Logan said as the flock of women moved toward the Tahoe.

25

"Back to see that old grump of a grandpa?" one of the other women asked.

Logan's jaw clenched, and he turned toward Tom.

Tom exhaled. "Cadillac Ranch is remote," he said under his breath, too quietly for the women to hear. "We've been able to keep the...what happened hushed for now."

Logan gave a nod.

"Okay, ladies. We need to go," Tom said. "You all have a nice day now." He accelerated slowly but deliberately and rolled the window up in sync. The gaggle of ladies finally took the hint and shuffled their way into Melvin's.

Logan sat back against the seat separating them, his neck stiff. She rested her hand on his shoulder.

Tom glanced over but looked away just as fast.

"How much longer do you think you can keep it quiet?" Logan asked, his voice hoarse.

Tom looked at the clock on the dash. "I'd say less than an hour now that they've seen you."

"They'll assume his grandfather is dead simply because he's here?" Em asked, her nose scrunched.

"They'll be taking 'welcome home' goodies out to the ranch for Logan as fast as their legs will carry them, and once they get there, they'll see..." Tom cleared his throat. "They'll understand."

Tom pulled to the next crosswalk, stopped, then made a left, heading away from the curving foothills and into the station lot not two blocks back.

Once they were parked, Logan hopped out and strode to get Em's door. He held her hand as she stepped down from the Tahoe, her skirt swirling about her legs in the wicked wind. "Is it always this—" she asked.

"Yes," both men said in unison.

"Santa Ana winds hit every October through March.

February is about the worst of it," Logan said, clutching her hand and guiding her toward the door as tumbleweeds barreled by. Logan tugged her to him, helping her avoid one hitting her straight on. "Tumbleweeds," he said.

"I pictured them being only in old Westerns."

"Nope." Logan chuckled. "Daily part of life here."

Tom reached the door first and held it open, his cowboy hat tipped down, the wind and dust blowing right off the rim. She was getting a glimmer of their use beyond looking attractive on a man. She wondered if Logan had one and how handsome he'd look wearing it, though picturing Mr. Dapper in a cowboy hat and jeans seemed so odd.

"Come on back," Tom said, leading them around the corner to where three brown desks sat. He clicked on his space heater. "Even the desert gets chilly in February—especially up in the mountains here in Cauldron Creek."

"Charlene," Logan said with a polite nod to the thirty-something, slender brunette.

"Hey, Logan." She stood. "I was so sorry to hear..." Her brown eyes misted with tears. "I'm sorry."

"Thanks, Charlene. I appreciate it."

"Charlene, this is Emmalyne Thorton—she's with the Coast Guard Investigative Service, like Logan. Special Agent Thorton," Tom said, "this is Charlene. She basically does everything around here and keeps me sane."

"Oh, I wouldn't say that," Charlene said. "Don't know that anyone would deem you sane." She smirked.

"This is Mable," Tom said, gesturing to the stocky blonde at the far desk.

"Ma'am. Logan." Mable greeted them with a nod.

"Pleased to meet both of you," Em said.

"Mable is our dispatcher..." Tom kept his attention on her. "Anything other than Ms. Baca's dog come in?"

"Another domestic disturbance out at the Wright ranch. Denton took the call."

"Thanks, Mable."

"Let's head in my office," he said, gesturing to the door straight back, *County Sherriff Mahoney* painted in black on the stubble glass. He reached for the burnished knob, opening the door, once again holding it open for Em and Logan to pass through.

"Take a seat," he said, removing his cowboy hat and setting it on the hat rack.

Logan held out a chair, and Em took the seat, Logan taking the chair beside her.

"We'll have you do the sketch as soon as Denton returns," Tom said, then he shifted forward, resting his forearms on the desk. "I know you want the facts...or you think you want the facts, but this isn't an objective case for you. It could be..."

"Painful," Em said, squeezing Logan's hand.

He squeezed back, but his expression didn't shift—he looked as resolute as always. "The best I can do by Colt is to give my all in any way I can to help you catch the killer."

Tom opened his top drawer, pulled out a file, and after a moment's hesitation, slid it across the desk.

Logan reached for it, but Tom kept his fingers braced on top. "Let me at least pull the crime scene photos," he said. "They aren't necessary."

Logan looked at his watch. "Has the scene been cleared?"

"The field investigator marked, photographed, and worked the scene, then once it was all done, he removed the markers, took the evidence to the crime lab, and transported Colt to the ME's office in Albuquerque." He glanced back at Em. "It's the only ME office in the state. Whenever a homicide happens, the bod—" Tom swallowed. "Sorry, man. The deceased go there."

"It's okay," Logan said. "Work the case like you normally would, talk like you normally would."

Em met Tom's gaze. Clearly, they were both thinking the same thing. Just because Logan was law enforcement and knew how cases worked didn't negate the fact someone he dearly loved had been murdered. There was a deep, personal connection in play whether he thought he could be objective or not.

"When can we look at what's left at the scene?" Logan asked.

Tom shifted, his chair squeaking beneath him. "There's no need since all the evidence was photographed and noted in the case file." He finally removed his hand from the manila folder.

Em swallowed. "Maybe you should let me..."

Logan arched a brow in that way that meant *no*. An emphatic no.

She sat back and crossed her legs. She'd never understood the expression "stubborn as the day is long" until she'd met Logan James Perry. He was the epitome of stubborn. He claimed the same of her, but he was wrong—as usual.

"I still want to see the scene," Logan said.

SIX

L ogan leaned forward. "We can be of the most help if we see the scene itself."

Tom inhaled. "All right, but let me have the service clean it up first."

"That would defeat the purpose."

"Logan—" Tom hesitated.

"You might as well give in now," Em said. "He's not gonna let this go."

Tom shook his head. "I see she knows you well."

Logan ignored both of them and opened the file. He immediately wished he hadn't as he stared at Colt's body, slumped against the wall, his stomach covered in blood. The killer had used a shotgun, and by the extent of damage, it'd been at close range. A stomach wound was an excruciating and brutally slow death. Heat pulsated through his body at the thought of what his grandpa had suffered.

"Logan," Em said.

"I'm fine."

"I'm going to give you two time to look through everything.

I'll be back in when Denton's here," Tom said, striding to the door.

"Thank you." Em nodded.

Tom slipped out and shut the door behind him.

"Logan," she said, resting her delicate hand on his arm.

"I'm fine, Em." He gripped the picture tightly, blood pulsing through his fingers.

"You're shaking," she said.

"She shot him in the stomach with a shotgun at close range."

A slight gasp escaped Em's lips. "Oh, Logan. I'm..."

He handed her the top photograph, his fingers nearly numb from his grip.

She looked down, tears welling in her eyes for a man she didn't know beyond the stories he'd told her. She had compassion. The woman who shot Colt clearly had none.

"Sheriff," Denton said, swiping into the office, stopping short at the sight of them. "Logan?"

Logan swallowed, forced himself to release Em's hand, and stood. "Denton." He nodded.

Denton's gaze shifted to Emmy. A smile crept on his lips until his gaze fixed on the photograph in her hand. "What are you doing?" He stepped forward and reached for it. "Excuse me, ma'am. This is confidential case information. If the sheriff knew—"

"It's all right, Denton," Tom said from the door as he leaned against the frame.

Denton's gaze swung to Tom. "Excuse me?"

Tom pushed off the doorframe and strode into his office, two paper coffee cups in hand. He offered one to Em.

"Thanks," she said, her astute gaze clearly taking in the nuances surrounding her. She was always good with vibes, had a gift of understanding the subtle looks, the choice of words, the unspoken relationship between two—or in this case, three —people.

Tom handed Logan the other cup, and he nodded, retaking his seat beside Em as Tom took his behind his desk. "It's okay, Denton. I'm giving them professional courtesy on the case."

Denton shifted his stance. "Sheriff, this isn't right. It's his grandpa. He can't be impartial."

"Impartial, no, but he's still a talented investigator," Tom said. "He and his colleague." He gestured to Em. "This is Special Agent Emmalyne Thorton. She will be a strong addition to our team on this."

"Our team?" Denton scoffed, raking a hand through his winged-back hair.

Logan bit back the harsh words stirring to rush out. Flashes of high school and their baseball team shot through his mind. Was Denton really that insecure still? Was he afraid he and Em would solve the case instead of him? He took a sip of coffee to temper his frustration. He wouldn't overstep Tom's boundaries out of respect, but he wasn't being benched.

Denton shifted his weight and shook his head. "Sheriff, now don't you think that's going too far? I know you're friends and all, but..."

"I've made up my mind," Tom said.

"How do you even know what kind of investigator he is? You're just taking his word for it?"

Tom nodded. "Logan and I discuss and brainstorm cases frequently when we want a sounding board. I know what an excellent investigator he is. Not to mention, his boss called to express what valuable assets these two will be to our investigation."

"These two, huh?" Denton's gaze grazed over Emmy.

Logan stiffened. If Denton even—

"She's a special agent, and I know you will treat her as such," Tom said.

"Of course." Denton smiled, one that bordered on a leer.

What was wrong with him? Colt had just been murdered, and Denton was still throwing hissy fits and leering at Em? Some men never grew up.

"Good," Tom said, "then back to the matter at hand. Denton, this is your lucky day."

Denton's brows furrowed. "Why's that?"

"Logan is his team's sketch artist. No need for us to wait on one from Albuquerque."

Denton shifted his stance, cocking his head. "We don't have supplies here."

"Logan's are in his knapsack," Em said, "he doesn't travel without them."

He sketched far more than criminals and unidentified missing persons. He sketched to breathe when the night crept in on him.

"Why don't you grab your gear?" Tom said, tossing Logan the patrol vehicle's keys.

He stood, giving Em a squeeze on the shoulder before stepping in front of Denton and standing firm. He wasn't budging—and apparently, neither was Denton, not yet. After a moment of holding his gaze, Denton stepped back, and Logan headed out for the patrol SUV.

The wind whipping the mesa in swirls about him whistled like a lone coyote, the sun moving higher in the sky, warming away any remaining hint of the cold night air as he stepped back inside and found Tom in the hall.

"I thought it would give you more space if you did this in the interrogation room," he said.

Logan looked through the two-way mirror. Denton sat with his back to the window, his legs sprawled out. His arms shifted

33

from crossed to uncrossed to the chair arms. The man was visibly seething, but Logan didn't care. He didn't need Denton to be happy—he just needed him to cooperate so they could solve this case. Whatever it took.

"Em?" he asked, not seeing her.

"Still in my office," Tom said. "I thought she and I could go over the case file in more depth while you work on the sketch."

"All right." Em would fill him in later. She would probably try to spare him some of the intimate details or graphic photos, but it was too late for that. That first picture had told him all he needed to know—and then some. He'd see Colt like that in his nightmares, even the waking ones.

"Denton," he said, stepping inside the interrogation room and closing the door behind him.

Denton's arms locked over his chest, and he remained reclined, long legs stretched out, one cowboy boot crossed over the other at his ankles.

Logan pulled out his pad and charcoal pencils. "Let's get started. Take a deep breath and—"

"I know how this works."

"Great. Then you know to take a deep breath, close your eyes, and picture what you saw of her."

"Sketchy eyes," Denton answered, his own eyes still open.

"Sketchy?"

"Yeah, darting about, trying not to let me see her. But it was too late. She'd stepped out of the bunkhouse without that hoodie on, and I saw her plain as day." Denton cracked his knuckles. "I am sorry about Colt," he said, much to Logan's surprise. "He was a good man."

Logan nodded his thanks—and his agreement. Colt was a far better man than he'd ever be, and yet he'd been senselessly gunned down, and for what? A few stolen items? Thanks to

Tom, he and Em had a lot of work cut out for them, but this sketch came first.

Since her eyes were what was most memorable to Denton, that was where they started.

"They were gaunt, black-rimmed," Denton said. "Like a junkie's."

"You think she was using drugs?"

"I'd bet on it. Probably why she kept that hoodie on, didn't make eye contact, kept her arms covered by the hoodie's sleeves."

"Colt would have kicked her out if he knew."

"I believe that," Denton said, shifting in his chair.

"Maybe he figured it out and told her to leave. Or maybe she decided to rob him for drug money, and he interrupted the robbery. It could be that she came in shooting, but at such close range, I'd wager she took her time. It's all supposition, of course, but it's an angle to pursue."

"Agreed." Denton nodded. "We should hear back on the evidence before too long. Hopefully, it'll provide more answers."

Logan prayed so as he continued with the sketch. The woman's eyes took shape and definition thanks to Denton's description, and before long, they'd moved on to her overall facial structure, filling in each feature and finally adding her hair to round the picture out.

He sat back and showed Denton.

"Dang, you aren't half bad," Denton said.

"You did a good job describing," Logan said.

Denton nodded. The self-important veneer he typically kept in place cracked a little and a slip of true sympathy was silently extended. Rubbing his thighs, he got to his feet. "Well, I better get that sketch out on the BOLO to state law enforcement agencies."

Logan nodded, taking one last look before handing it over to Denton. Looking into the woman's haunting eyes—the droopy eyes of a junkie—had sucked the breath from his lungs, but he'd stared until he had them memorized.

One glance into her eyes, and he'd have Colt's killer.

SEVEN

Following breakfast on the go, Tom turned onto a dirt road. The sun's brilliant sunbeams fanned out across the beautiful land, shining in hues of coral and rust as it rose even higher in the sky. She'd managed to sleep on their flights and woke up slightly before dawn in another world.

The land... She crinkled her nose. What had Logan called it? Not desert. Something else.

Mesa. That was it—the mesa. And it was stunning, stretching as far as she could see—all the way to the horizon. The blue sky was so bright and clear, even through the Tahoe's window. It was spectacular.

The road ended in a driveway, and they pulled to a stop.

She waited, anticipating stepping out, but both Logan and Tom remained in their bucket seats. She squeezed her eyes shut on a prayer.

Please help him, Lord. Wrap Your arms of love around him as he endures this tragedy.

When she opened her eyes, she trailed her gaze along the large terra-cotta-colored rancher with yellow-and-black crime scene tape stretched across the carved wooden door. She swallowed. Logan's head hadn't turned toward the house yet. Was that on purpose?

Instead, his gaze remained on a steel pen on his side of the vehicle.

She turned her attention back to what had been Logan's home, trying to reconcile *Mr. Dapper,* who always wore the well-tailored suits and Jimmy Choo shoes, with the rugged environment surrounding them. She looked back at the house, at the raw-hewn beams supporting the flat roof extending over the porch. Four wooden rockers spread out across it, and a cowbell hung in place of windchimes, which made her smile until she caught Logan's glance toward the house. She didn't need to see the expression on his face to feel his heartache. It coursed through the vehicle, throbbing in her chest. The visceral weight of pain stabbing through her at his suffering nearly knocked the wind from her lungs.

"I'm so sorry," she said, leaning forward and resting her hand on his shoulder.

"I know," he said in a hoarse whisper. He raised his arm and rested his warm hand over hers. "Thanks for being here for me."

She'd always be there for him. But would he ever be there for her...like that? In the way her heart ached for?

She shook off the thoughts. Why did her feelings for Logan, and the question of his for her, continue to loop through her mind? Her thoughts and focus needed to be *fully* fixed on being here for Logan and working the case. Her feelings weren't relevant—not now.

Still, they remained in the vehicle, Tom and Logan silent, his hand still atop hers. She shifted forward, wanting to be closer to him—*for* him, she told herself.

Horses whinnied in the distance, breaking the stillness. She shifted her gaze back to the pen Logan had been staring at. A handful of horses came over the rise, loping to the fence.

"Well." Logan released a weighted sigh, his hand twitching on top of hers. "As Colt always said, time ain't going to pass itself."

Logan cracked his door, paused and then, with a sigh, climbed out and moved to open her door.

Her skirt whipped about her legs in the wild gusts as she climbed out. She'd have to see about getting some jeans. There weren't any in her go-bag. She didn't even own a pair, always preferring dresses and skirts to pants.

Following Logan around the rear of the vehicle, she feared her heels would sink in the ground that she'd imagined would feel like sand, but it turned out to be hard-packed with sunbaked cracks spidering out across the dried earth.

The horses whinnied in a flurry at the sight of Logan. One in particular—tan with a black mane and matching black socks—reared up on his back hooves, his front legs waving in the air before he stomped down, the mesa kicking up with his force.

"I see you, Bathtub," Logan said, a soft yet sorrowful smile gracing his lips.

Em arched a brow. "Did you just call him Bathtub?"

"Yep, but she's a girl. I'd best go say hi, or she won't stop. Are you okay for a minute?"

"Of course. Take your time."

He nodded and strode for the fence, then paused and looked over his shoulder, the sun lighting his soulful blue eyes. "You want to come meet her?"

"Sure." She glanced back to find Tom had gone to the porch and taken a seat in one of the rockers, one booted foot resting on the opposite knee.

"Take your time," he said when he caught her gaze.

She nodded with a smile.

He was a good guy and from everything she'd witnessed, a good friend to Logan.

It was funny to picture Logan with a guy friend outside of their CGIS team. Back home, he never really hung out with guys—only his girl of the month.

Her chest squeezed at the thought, then slowly loosened as she remembered that he hadn't dated in months.

"Em?" he said.

"Right. Sorry." She hurried to his side. She had to get out of her head—it was taking her to deep places, but right now, she needed to be fully present rather than wool-gathering.

Approaching the fence, Logan held his hand up, and she stopped a handful of feet from the pen.

"Let me settle her first," he said. "She's a jealous girl."

"Is that right?"

"Most definitely." The hint of a smile tugged at the corner of his mouth as he approached Bathtub. "Hey, girl. It's been too long, I know." She stopped rearing and he stroked her muzzle. She nudged him with her nose.

"I know." Sadness engulfed his voice. "I already miss him, too."

Em's heart splintered. She wanted to pull him in her arms and not let go until the pain subsided, but unfortunately, she didn't possess the power to heal that depth of hurt. Only God could bring the comfort he needed in the midst of anguish. Tears burned her eyes as she lifted her chin at Bathtub. "She loves you," she said. *And so do I.*

He nodded. It was clear he returned Bathtub's affection.

"Bucky's been taking good care of them," Tom hollered from the porch.

Glancing over her shoulder, she found him now standing and leaning against one of the raw-hewn beams. "But they know," he added, sorrow tinging his voice.

"She's too intelligent and perceptive not to," Logan said, continuing to stroke Bathtub's muzzle. He looked at Em. "Want to say hi before we head inside?"

"Yes, please." She enjoyed seeing the bond Logan had with Bathtub. She knew he'd grown up in the Southwest, but she hadn't pictured him being so in sync with animals, but to her surprise, it suited him.

"Come here," he said, holding out his hand.

She took hold.

"Nice and slow," he said, tugging her with tenderness to his side.

The horse's wide, almond-shaped eyes fixed on Emmy.

"Bathtub, this is Em. She's special," he added, "so be nice."

Special? She looked at him and he held her gaze. Was that love shining in his striking blue eyes?

"Here," he said, lifting her hand. "Like this," he said, covering her hand with his and running it down the horse's muzzle in soothing, rhythmic strokes.

"There you go," Logan said, lifting his hand off Em's.

She continued stroking, finding an unexpected peace in the movement.

The other horses in the pen whinnied.

"Hey, guys. Sorry. I see you, too," Logan said, stroking each of their muzzles in turn. "Here we have Wrangler, Stella, Bartholomew..." he said, introducing them to Em.

She arched a brow. *Bartholomew for a horse?* Though what kind of name was Bathtub?

"Colt's doing." Logan shrugged. "Oh, and this beauty," he said, reaching for a younger horse with a light coat and blonde mane, "is Stella's girl, Maverick."

"She's precious." And she loved the name Maverick for a girl.

They remained there, time slipping by, until Logan took a

stiff inhale and shucked his shoe against the dirt. "We'd best get to it," he said, stepping back.

Bathtub grumbled.

He offered her a soft smile, but it was filled with sorrow. "I'll be back, I promise."

She didn't look happy, but she settled as they stepped away.

Walking beside him toward the house, Em noted his countenance shifting from momentary solace to one of overwhelming sorrow.

"You sure you want to do this?" Tom asked, pushing off the beam as they approached.

"I have to." Logan swallowed beside her, his pronounced Adam's apple bobbing in his throat.

On a slow exhale, Tom peeled away crime scene tape. "You're sure?" he asked one more time, his hand on the door handle.

Logan nodded. He closed his eyes for a breath of a moment, his lips moving silently in prayer.

She closed her eyes and prayed God would grant them both strength. They were going to need it.

EIGHT

Tom opened the door, and Logan opened his eyes.

He steeled himself before he crossed over the threshold, knowing that the moments to come would alter his life forever.

Tom took off his hat and clutched it in his hand.

Light cracked through the wooden blinds, the air thick and stale with the metallic odor of blood. His stomach roiled, but he ignored the sloshing in his gut.

No matter how excruciating working Colt's crime scene became, he had to continue. For Colt.

He looked over at Em. They had a ninety-five percent closure rate on their CGIS cases. They could do this together, just like every other case they worked. But this was no other case. This was beyond personal.

"Vicks?" Tom asked, offering the jar to Emmy, who took a swipe and rubbed it under her nose. Logan followed suit, exhaling a little in relief as the brisk eucalyptus scent overpowered the stench of blood.

Clearing the torment from his throat—or at least attempting

to—he said, "Tom, could I have the crime scene photos?" He wanted to see where the collected evidence had lain, where the field investigator had put the markers before noting each item.

After a moment of hesitation, Tom handed the case file to him.

"Thanks," Logan said, then turned to Em.

She stepped to his side and took the remainder of the folder after he'd pulled the photographs out.

"Can I take some photographs of my own?" she asked Tom.

"I don't see why not. Technically, the crime scene will be considered cleared once Logan walks through the house and sees if anything else inside is missing other than Colt's gun. After that, the tape will come down and the house will be yours. But..." he added as Em pulled out her camera. "Don't move anything until we finish the walk-through."

"Understood," she said.

Logan handed her a pair of gloves from the pack Tom had given them at the station. Slipping them on, he snapped both at the wrist to secure them in place. Then they all slipped booties on in turn. There was a chance that he might spot something that triggered a need for a second visit from the field investigator, so all precautions had to be taken to preserve the scene.

"I'll get the shades," Tom said, rounding the corner of the foyer.

Logan looked to Em, and she nodded.

Taking a bracing breath, he prayed, *Lord, give me courage,* before following Tom into the living room where the murder had occurred.

With trepidation at what he'd find, he cast his gaze on the far wall as the sunlight beamed in through the open shades and the ceiling lights flicked on.

Blood spatter covered the back living room wall—reddish-brown blood, a stark contrast to the white surface. The point of impact held the most gore—splayed in a sort of misshapen circle. Spray marks fanned out from there, including a streak that trailed down to the ground where another dried puddle had pooled beneath the body and seeped out onto the surrounding tile floor.

Tom's assessment, as noted in the file, was that Colt had been standing in front of the wall when he was shot. After that, he slid down until he slumped against the ground and eventually died.

Anguish stabbed in sharp, piercing slashes at Logan's chest, stealing the breath from his lungs. He forced himself to draw in a breath, shallow as it was.

Based on the evidence, he'd say Tom had called everything right, which didn't surprise him. Tom was a talented investigator.

He sensed Em studying him as he moved about the scene, but she didn't ask any questions of him. He appreciated it. The bond between them was a strong, woven cord. She knew what he was thinking...experiencing. Somehow, she always had when it came to working cases. He was far from okay, and they both knew it, but speaking the words would only hinder his ability to maintain a professional façade in Tom's eyes. He had to work this case like any other, but he needed God's help to do so.

"A double-aught was pulled from the center of the blood spray," Tom said, taking a pencil from his pocket and circling the round hole in the wall. He straightened. "Are you sure you want to hear all of this?" he asked Logan.

"Yes."

"All right." Tom continued. "The field investigator said it's from the exit wound. The rest of the double-aught pellets that were lodged in the wall missed his body."

"So one exit wound?" Logan asked, needing to confirm the details.

"Yes," Tom agreed. "Given the two shells and the number of pellets, we know the shotgun was fired twice." Tom rubbed the back of his neck.

"Go on. I can take it," Logan said. In all honesty, he was unsure if he truly could, but he owed it to Colt to work this case to the best of his ability.

"Given there are eight pellets per shell, and taking the ones that hit the wall into account, at least five pellets hit him, four only partially perforating the body. Anyway, that's what the field investigator believes. We'll be able to confirm upon autopsy."

Logan curled his hands into fists, the blood circulation pooling hard in his scrunched fingers. He wanted to scream, fought not to cry. His poor grandpa had suffered. He'd hunt down whoever did this and see them behind bars if it was the last thing he did.

"Can I see the pictures?" Em asked, pulling his mind from the horrid image of Colt slumped on the floor, dying.

"I'd like to photograph all the areas marked," she continued. "With everything already collected, we'll need to go off the photographs."

"Here," Logan said, moving to her side, the photographs still in his hand. "I'll direct you."

Emmy crouched down, taking photographs while Logan relayed where each marker had stood. They both sank on their haunches, thoroughly examining each area. The only physical trace the field investigator had noted of the killer was a partial smeared, bloody shoe print.

Logan stood, stepping back and studying the rest of the tile. The partial was found a good thirty feet from where Colt's body had lain. To get blood on her shoe, the killer would have had to step in the blood pool. Step within a foot of Colt's body. Why?

The fact that there was only one bloody shoe print meant she'd taken time to clean other shoe prints up. No way she'd stepped in the blood pool and her shoes had only left one print. Had she simply missed scrubbing that one up in her rush to leave? Or had something kept her from noticing it?

"Could you pull the shades closed a moment?" he asked Tom.

Tom arched a brow. "S...ur...e." He moved for the blinds.

Once the blackout shades were drawn, the only illumination left was from the ceiling fan light. Logan turned the end table lamp on, knowing that those were the two lights Colt always kept on.

He stepped back, and Emmy did so in sync with him, both surveying the floor.

"A shadow falls on the partial," Em said.

He nodded, loving how they were always on the same wavelength.

"That's how she missed it," he said.

Em looked around. "The cowboy hat shelf is casting it," she said, then quirked her head, no doubt wondering why the hats on the shelf rested upside down.

"Wow. Your boss wasn't exaggerating. You guys *are* good," Tom said.

"Years of working together," Logan said, sinking down into a crouch by the dried partial. "I'm assuming the field investigator took an imprint?"

"Yes," Tom said, leaning against the kiva fireplace out of their way. "Denton photographed the scene when we arrived, but we left everything in place and untouched for the field investigator."

"Any idea when you can expect the report?" Logan asked.

"He said it can take a couple weeks." The crease on Tom's brow said he wasn't any more pleased with the delay than Logan was.

The one difficulty of living in a remote mountain town—anything needed from the outside world took time.

Logan turned to Em. "Looks like a woman's size ten to me... what do you think?" he asked of the reddish-brown print atop the terra-cotta floor tile.

Em pulled her pencil-thin flashlight from her crossbody bag that doubled as a purse and studied it. "I agree. It's a woman's size ten or a man's size eight-and-a-half."

"A woman's size ten?" Tom frowned. "That's a larger-than-average size."

"How tall was the woman?" Logan asked. He'd only sketched her face, so he hadn't asked Denton for any details about her height or frame.

"Denton said about five-four." Tom held his hand up to indicate the height.

"And weight?" Em asked.

"About your size," Tom said to Em.

Logan glanced over at her and arched a brow.

"You're not supposed to ask a woman her weight, but in this case, it's warranted. I weigh one hundred and thirty, but I'm five-seven," so if she looks my size, she probably weighs less."

"Okay, so one-thirty at the most, probably a bit less," Logan said. "Not what I'd expect from someone who'd have a larger shoe size."

"So, is it possible we're looking at someone else's print?" Em asked. "A man's, possibly? Though eight-and-a-half is on the smaller size for a man."

Logan looked to Tom. "Bucky found Colt, correct?"

"Correct. Like I mentioned, he was bringing Colt some of Caroline's biscochitos when he found him."

"Is it possible it's Bucky's shoeprint?" Logan asked. Had he stepped in the blood pool before Tom and Denton arrived?

"Bucky was frozen at the edge of the living room when we arrived. He was staring wide-eyed, all shaken up."

"Did Bucky touch anything?"

Tom shook his head. "No. Bucky left the body undisturbed. He saw that Colt was beyond help and couldn't bring himself to get any closer. He just remained fixed on the edge of the room."

"So not Bucky's, yours, or Denton's shoeprint," Logan said, helping Em to her feet.

"If we're right about the size of the print," Em began, "she either had a larger-than-average foot for a woman of her build, or..."

"Or someone else was present," Logan said.

NINE

Em followed Logan as he walked through Colt's home —*his* home from a young age. She still didn't know why he'd lived with his grandfather rather than his parents. She'd never asked. He'd share if he wanted to. So far, that hadn't been the case.

Finishing with the living room and not finding anything else missing there, she and Tom followed Logan down the hall to their left. All the while, the realization that a second person could have been present during the shooting hung thick in the air.

Whose shoe print was it? *Had* someone else been there? Had the drifter known someone local or met with someone on the outskirts of town? Denton had said she'd borrowed Colt's pickup, but no one saw her in town or knew where she went. Was someone else involved in Colt's death—or did the woman really have a size-ten foot?

Logan paused outside a door, his gloved hand on the knob.

"Colt's room?" she asked, tears pricking at her eyes at the anguish on Logan's face.

He nodded. After another moment's pause, he pushed the door open. It creaked on its hinges, and a shiver slithered down Em's spine. The entire room was asunder.

Logan took a stiff inhale.

Two dressers stood on opposite walls—one long horizontally with six drawers, the other tall with five drawers. Each one was pulled out and dumped on the floor, clothes and other personal items discarded everywhere. Dark-hued material streaked across the cream carpet. Watches lay about them, glistening in the ceiling fan light. Coins and old photographs—the square black-and-white ones with white borders—had been tossed across the dresser top and onto the floor.

Logan bent, retrieving one. Clasping it in his hands, tears beaded in his eyes as red flushed his face.

Em yearned to pull him in her arms and would have had they been alone.

"We figure she was looking for a few high-value items that would be easy to pawn," Tom said from the doorway. "We're guessing she didn't consider the watches valuable enough."

Logan turned to face his friend; the photograph still clutched in his hand. "Okay to take this?" he asked.

Tom nodded as he entered the room, and Logan slipped it in his shirt pocket before Em could see it.

She wondered who the subject of it was, and why that one photograph out of so many tossed about meant more to him.

Logan bent, examining the watches. "His Breitling is missing—unless he was wearing it, but I didn't notice it in the crime scene photos."

"No watch on him when he was found," Tom said, leaning against the wall. "Although, she could have taken it off of him."

Nausea rumbled in Emmy's stomach, and she swallowed the queasiness at the thought. How could someone murder an elderly man and then possibly possess the depth of cruelty needed to steal something off of him while he lay dying? If that had been the case, the killer would have had to step close to Colt—mortally wounded and in agonizing suffering—and snatch the watch right off his wrist.

"I've got to ask..." Tom said. "What kind of watch is a Breitling?"

"It's a pilot's watch. It's got the bidirectional, rotating bezel to control the iconic aviation slide rule."

"I didn't know your grandpa was a pilot," Em said.

"Yep. He owns...owned a biplane kept over at the local runway."

"He's not the only pilot in the family," Tom said, inclining his head toward Logan.

"You fly?" Em asked. Here she thought she knew everything about Logan.

He nodded.

Now wasn't the time for a deeper conversation, but later she wanted to hear all about his flying.

"How much is a watch like that worth?" Tom asked.

"About nine grand," Logan said.

Tom's jaw slackened. "Seriously?"

"It was a Christmas gift."

It didn't surprise her that he'd spent so much. Logan was a trust fund kid since his mom passed when he was young, so money was rarely an issue for him, and she knew he liked to treat the people he cared about. If there was one thing Logan was, it was generous.

"From you?" Tom's eyes remained wide.

Logan nodded. "For Christmas." Sadness drenched his tone. "I guess it was the last gift I gave him."

"Oh, honey," Em said, forgetting Tom was even present— her full attention rapt on the man she loved. A man wading deep in sorrow's clutches.

"I should have come sooner," he said, his gaze fixed on the ground.

"You couldn't have known," she whispered.

His hands balled into fists. "Now it's too late."

"I wonder how the drifter knew to take the watch," Tom said, clearly trying to pull Logan's attention off his evident regret and onto the case. The investigation gave him purpose and it would keep him from falling headlong into grief. He'd still grieve but he had an outlet to funnel it through. A killer to put behind bars.

Logan released a jagged exhale, "I suppose she saw that it stood out," he said, finally answering his friend's question.

Tom's features were composed, though a sadness hung in his brown eyes—had been there since he'd picked them up at the airport. "Anything else missing?" he asked.

"Let me look through the jewelry box." Logan bent, pulling a white, leather box out of one of the discarded drawers. "This is where Colt kept my grandma's and Aunt Rae's things after they both passed." He opened it and pulled the inset tiers up.

A handful of moments later, Logan assured them nothing else was missing, but then he hesitated. "Except..." he said, setting the jewelry box on top of the dresser and moving for another of the tossed drawers. "I forgot the puzzle box."

"Puzzle box?" Intrigue sifted through Em. She loved solving puzzles.

"Colt had a thing for puzzles and hidden spots," Tom said, still holding up the wall.

"He's right. Colt kept things in secret places, and Tom and I were always on the lookout for them. He thought it was a fun game." Logan rummaged through the drawer, then pulled out a box with a checkerboard pattern in two different shades of wood. "A piece is out of place." He scrambled to open it, and his face paled.

"What's wrong?" Em asked. "What's missing?

"She took Mee-Maw's wedding ring," he choked out.

"Oh, Logan." She stepped closer, wanting to be near him. What she really wanted was to pull him in her arms and heal the pain etched across his handsome face, but they needed to maintain some level of professionalism with Tom present.

Logan looked at Tom. "We have to get it back."

"We will," Tom said. "Denton sent a copy of her sketch out to local authorities as well as to all the pawn shops in our county and the surrounding ones. If she is a junkie, she's going to want to pawn the ring and watch for cash fast. "

Logan nodded, closed the puzzle box in three moves, then set it atop the tall dresser.

Tom pushed off the wall. "We should check your room and the guest room."

Em followed the men back into the hall, curious what Logan's childhood room would be like.

Entering the guest room first, Logan cleared it of any missing items. "Looks like nothing's been touched or moved."

"Maybe she bypassed it," Em said.

Logan strode for the door, then turned back, his gaze sweeping the full room. "I wonder if she cased the house ahead of time. It appears like she knew where to look and *what* to look for."

"I agree," Tom said, then looked to Logan. "Your room?"

Logan nodded and led the way to the door at the end of the hall. Opening it, he gestured Em and Tom inside, then followed.

The lights were off, the shades closed. It was hard to make out much.

Logan flipped the light switch and two lamps turned on, bathing the room in a soft glow. "I'll get the shades too," he said, striding for them. He pulled the string and sunlight came streaming in, beams dashing across the evergreen comforter on the king-size bed.

Em took in the carved, wooden headboard. It was a Biblical scene of Daniel in the Lion's den, and it was breathtaking handiwork.

"Nothing looks out of place," Logan said, turning to Tom. "I think your supposition that she'd cased the place is a sound one. It definitely appears like she knew where to look and what she wanted to take."

Em's chest squeezed, her breath growing shallow as it all raced through her mind. Why would anyone murder someone over a few stolen items? It made no sense...and yet she'd seen it happen in her line of work multiple times. Degrading the sanctity of human life for money—often a meager amount.

"So...she cased the place," Tom began. "Came in to rob it. Colt interrupted her and she shot him."

"Or," Logan said. "She came in shooting, but why?" His brow furrowed in that way it always did when he was in deep contemplation on a case.

"Maybe she had a secondary motive for killing Colt?" Em said, thinking out loud.

"Such as?"

"A cover-up," she offered as scenarios continued racing through her mind.

"Cover-up for what?" Logan volleyed back.

She loved how they worked so seamlessly together, tossing out ideas and then building off of them. "Maybe she wanted it to look like an interrupted robbery."

"Possible," Logan said, pacing the hardwood floor. "Three scenarios..."

"But which is right?" Em asked.

Tom's gaze bounced between them. "You guys have your own language, don't you?"

"Em presents every angle a crime could have taken, even the less obvious ones," Logan explained.

"And Logan figures out which one is right," she said, rocking back on her heels.

"*We* figure out which is right," he said.

"Okay, so three options," Tom said, nudging them to continue.

Em gestured for Logan to run with it as she leaned against the side of a rough-hewn bookcase filled with westerns, mysteries, and shelves of history books.

"One," Logan began. "Colt interrupted the woman robbing him, and she shot him. Two, she came to rob him and shot him first to get him out of the way. Or three, she came to kill him, and the robbery was either a secondary action or a cover-up." He looked to Em. "Have I got it right?"

"Yep." She nodded.

"Now..." Logan's jaw set, "we investigate to determine which option is true."

"Just remember you're here on courtesy," Tom said. "You keep me in the loop, and I'll share as I'm able."

"Roger that." Logan nodded. "Oh...I've a question. It just hit me, but there wasn't anything in the case file about signs of a struggle. I know Colt, and he wouldn't just stand there and let her rob him. Nor would he stand still if she pulled a gun on him. Not in his house."

"Agreed." Tom gave a nod.

"So she came in shooting?" Em said. "Not giving him time to react?"

"The distance from the wall where he was found and the entry to the living room is thirty feet. We placed the shots as being fired from a distance of around ten to fifteen feet."

"Feet..." Logan said, rubbing his chin still smattered with yesterday's five o'clock shadow.

Em furrowed her brow. "What is it?"

"Colt was on his feet, standing by the wall halfway between his recliner and the TV."

"*Jeopardy.*" Tom snapped his fingers.

She looked between the two men. Now she was the lost one.

"Colt always watched *Jeopardy*. Channel 13 at six p.m. and then *Wheel of Fortune*," Logan explained. "With the time of death, he should have been in his recliner."

"So she entered. He stood, most likely moving for his gun in the display case on his bookshelves, and she shot him before he could reach it, firing twice." The muscle in Tom's clenched jaw twitched.

"It makes the most sense," Logan said, and she agreed.

"Now the question is why?" Em said. "Was it just to rob him? Or was something more sinister at play?"

TEN

Running through the possibilities of the crime had flipped Logan's stomach and sent a chill spidering up his neck. She'd invaded their home, invaded the space that had always been so safe and welcoming to him. That safety had been shattered, and the person who had made this home so welcoming was gone forever. The thought sent heat and pain coursing through his constricting limbs.

He walked the perimeter of his room, pausing at the sketch he'd done of Em on his last visit home. He swallowed and looked over his shoulder at her.

She stood, her eyes transfixed on it. After a moment, she blinked, her gaze flickering to him. Moisture brimmed in her beautiful green eyes.

"I'm..." Tom cleared his throat. "I'm going to do another round in the living room." He hightailed it out of there before either he or Em could speak.

"It's beautiful," she said, eyes wide.

He nodded his thanks, wanting to keep studying her face and the surprise welling in her eyes—but he needed to finish clearing the room despite it looking untouched. "I better get back to it," he said.

"Of course." She took a step back. "Actually..." She tugged at her ear.

Her nervous tell. Was she nervous? Had his sketch made her so?

"I'll go help Tom," she muttered.

He arched a brow. "You sure?"

"Yeah. You've got this." She turned and left as fast as Tom had.

Ten minutes later, Logan caught up with them in the living room. "There's nothing missing in my room, either."

"All right," Tom said. "So just to confirm. From the house, we have Colt's revolver, his Breitling watch, and your Mee-Maw's ring. Am I missing anything?"

"That's everything—unless she took cash," he said. "Colt always kept a fair amount in the house," he explained to Em.

"The ME called while you were in your room," Tom began. "He said when he searched Colt's clothes for evidence, his pockets were empty."

A wave of unease rushed over Logan, his limbs quivering. "Is his autopsy happening now?"

Tom nodded, then hung his head.

Logan gripped the chairback beside him for stability.

"Logan..." Em said, striding to him, concern evident in her eyes. "You okay?"

"Yeah. It just hit me." The fierce reality of it.

Em's face softened with deep compassion. "I'm so sorry."

He nodded, fighting back the tears pricking at his eyes. He sniffed, shifting his thoughts to the case. "If his money clip wasn't in his jeans' pocket, she must have taken that, too." He gripped the chair harder, the carved wood biting into his flesh. She'd taken money and most likely his watch off

59

him as he lay dying. What kind of monster were they dealing with?

"I'll add it to the report," Tom said.

He opened his eyes on an inhale. "And we should check the book. See if any cash is missing."

"Right," Tom said. "I didn't think about the empty book."

Em's eyes narrowed. "Empty book?"

Logan headed straight for the bookcases lining the side wall and pulled the faux-classic novel from the shelf. He opened the hollowed-out box and tipped it over. A wad of cash—and a thin roll of paper tucked inside the wad—tumbled out. "Apparently, she didn't know to look here, either," he said, bending to pick up the cash and return it to the box, but then he paused at the slip of paper. His hands still gloved, he picked it up and unrolled it. Colt was always tucking notes and reminders away in his "memory" spots. It'd begun as a way to get Logan to communicate after being dropped off on his grandpa's porch by a father who never looked back. Entrenched in pain from what had happened—from what he'd done—Logan didn't speak for his first weeks on the ranch. Colt's codes and secret messages gradually brought him back, but the pain never fully subsided. He doubted it ever would.

"What's it say?" Tom asked, taking a step closer.

"It's one of his codes," Logan said, shifting his full focus back on it. "Two rows of numbers..." He rolled the paper up and tucked it back in with the cash, returning it to the bookshelf. Now was not the time for games.

"We've got the bunkhouse left to go through," Tom said.

Where Colt's killer had stayed. The heat of anger flushed through him anew. Colt had let her stay and... Logan cut off the thought, reminding himself to focus. Going into the bunkhouse three shades of furious wouldn't help him be objective. Not that he really thought he had any chance of staying objective, but Em could. He'd rely on her to help him see what he might miss.

"After you check the bunkhouse for any missing items, I'll call the cleaning service for you. See how fast they can come out."

"Thanks, Tom, but I'll handle it." If something needed to be done, Colt had taught him, you rolled up your sleeves and set to work.

"Logan." Concern hung thick in Tom's voice. "Don't do that to yourself."

Tom didn't understand. "I owe it to him."

"He would have wanted you to hire a service. He wouldn't want you to have to...you know..." Tom shrugged.

"Maybe we can talk outside a moment," Em said, looking at him with equal concern in her gaze.

"We'd best go through the bunkhouse first," he said, knowing only Em had the power to talk him out of something.

She nodded, but the set of her jaw said this conversation wasn't over.

Tom led the way to the bunkhouse. The horses whinnied in the distance as they made the half-mile haul to the row of three white, clapboard bunkhouses.

"She stayed in the first one," Tom said. "That's where Denton got a look at her."

"Denton said she was as skittish as a prairie dog when the coyotes descend at night. He engaged her, she rushed out a greeting and headed back in the bunkhouse as fast as she could."

"I wonder why she was so jumpy, so afraid to be seen," Em said. "Maybe she really was running from someone like an ex."

"Or running from the law." Tom opened the bunkhouse door. "We didn't note any personal items of hers in the bunkhouse, but it would be good for you to take a second look.

We might have thought something belonged to the bunkhouse when it was something she'd brought in."

"I'm confused." Logan frowned as the case file notes streamed back through his mind.

Tom's brows furrowed. "About what?"

"I didn't see anything in the case file about prints...her prints."

Tom gestured them inside. Once they were standing in a tight circle in the limited floor space of the bunkhouse, he said, with a rub of his neck, "There weren't any."

Logan blinked. It hadn't hit him initially. The crime scene photos had saturated his mind, but how...? "How is that possible?"

"She must have wiped down the bunkhouse and worn gloves in Colt's home."

"So she went in prepared for what happened," Em said. "That lines up with her going in shooting."

Tom shrugged. "Looks that way."

"If she was worried about leaving prints, she's probably got a record," Logan said.

"Agreed." Tom scooted further in, giving them more elbow room. "Hopefully now that we've gotten the sketch circulating, we'll get some hits. I'm praying someone has at least seen her."

"She clearly wasn't local." Logan turned to Em to elaborate. "If she was local, the entire town of Cauldron Creek would be able to identify her." Small towns had their perks...as well as their cons.

"I'm thinking she's a city girl or that she came from somewhere on the fringes of one." Tom folded a piece of gum into his mouth.

"The closest large city is Albuquerque, right?" Em asked.

"Yes, ma'am," Tom said.

"You and I are going to have to get one thing straight," she said in that unyielding voice. "It's Emmy to you."

"Yes, m—" Tom hitched. "Emmy," he corrected.

"Better," she said. "So you're thinking Albuquerque? Is that where you're going to focus your attention?"

"Yes, I believe so. Denton's on his way there now to observe what he can of the autopsy, but he'll only catch the very end—if that. But he'll do some investigating while he's there in coordination with local police."

"And the evidence the ME gathered?" Logan asked.

"The ME bagged the evidence and will give chain of custody to Denton for him to examine the items and then take them over to the crime lab."

Logan longed to go himself, to be the one to take care of all aspects of Colt's investigation, but Denton was already there. Maybe that was a good thing. Seeing his grandpa's autopsy would break him.

"Denton will also canvas the bus stations in Albuquerque and the surrounding towns that have one. But Albuquerque isn't the only city option," Tom said.

"No?" Em arched a brow.

"No." Logan shook his head. "Phoenix is only a couple hours further than Albuquerque is."

"Oh." Em bit her bottom lip. "So she could have gone either way?"

"Unless she's headed for the border." Logan exhaled, praying she hadn't made it across if that was where she was headed.

ELEVEN

"As I mentioned, we put up barricades outside of town, but..." Tom said, continuing the conversation.

"But she was probably long gone by then, right?" Logan said, his tone respectful.

"By the time it was all in place..." Tom glanced down, then back up. "Yeah, I'm afraid that's most likely the case."

"Unless she's hiding nearby," Em said, and both men swiveled their heads toward her.

"Come again?" Tom said.

"I believe she knew someone nearby. She borrowed the truck for a reason. We know it wasn't to go to town," Em continued, "so, to me, it just makes sense that she was going to see someone."

"Probably to score drugs," Tom said.

"Agreed," Em said, "but working all the angles again, what if it's something more? Say she knew someone in the area—not in town, but on the outskirts. Somewhere she could drive to and be back before Colt started to wonder about her being gone too long. We shouldn't rule out that possibility. And if it *is* true, then that gives us another option for where she could have gone."

"She could be hiding out with them," Tom said. "Excellent point. I'll start canvassing the extended area while Denton is in Albuquerque."

Logan looked to the room they still had to clear.

Tom's cell rang. "Shoot," he said, glancing at the incoming number. "I've got to take this. You guys okay?"

"Yep," Em said.

"I'll be right back." Tom stepped out the door, taking the call. His voice wafted through the closed bunkhouse door, but it was too muffled to make out words.

Em's gaze swept over the bunkhouse. "How does it look to you?"

"Lived in. The chair in the corner has been moved, looks like so she could put her feet up on the bed."

"Could it have been moved before she got here?"

"Colt set things up a certain way and didn't bother changing anything unless there was a specific purpose."

"Gotcha."

"Sorry, folks." Tom stepped back in.

"Any news?" Logan asked.

"Not on Colt's case." Tom left it there. He gestured to the bed with a lift of his chin. "She stripped it. Must have taken all the bedding with her."

Logan blinked. "What on earth?"

"Weird, right?" Tom said.

Em studied the bare mattress. "I guess she was clearing anything that could provide physical evidence. A bed's kind of impossible to wipe down."

Shaking his head at the extent of the precautions the woman had taken, he got to work and quickly cleared the small bunkhouse. They were out the door when he stopped on the second step down.

Em looked back. "What's up?"

"The message hole," Logan said.

Em's brows arched. "There's one in here, too?"

"There's one in every building," Tom said. "I was so focused on the main physical evidence that I didn't think to look in them. This is why it's always good for a family member to do a walk-through. We think big picture, they think minutia."

Logan moved back inside and climbed up on the mattress with Tom's okay. He removed the painting from the wall and handed it to Tom.

With a press of his hand in the corner of the hidden panel, it pushed in. He reached into the opening, his hand curling around a bundle. Grabbing it, he hopped down and opened it up on the bed. Staring at the contents, he froze.

"What is it?" Tom looked over his shoulder. "Oh."

"What's wrong?" Em asked.

It was a leftover package from one of their games. The codes his grandfather had written, the cipher they'd used to break the code, a compass Colt had given him, and a few other items that had been of great significance to him as a child. A boy's treasure trove. "I didn't realize this was still here."

"It's probably been years since we last pulled it out," Tom said. "It's easy to forget."

Logan nodded and balled it back up, reaffixing the knot to hold everything in place. "Okay if I take it into the house...into my room?"

"Of course," Tom said. "But speaking of your room, have you thought about where y'all are going to stay until the house is ready?"

At some point, he'd need to stay in the house again. It was

his and Colt's home. He wasn't abandoning it. But knowing what happened to Colt in it...having seen the crime scene...he would not rest easy. Not for a long while.

"We can stay in Aunt Rae's place for now," he said. Colt had kept his sister's place up for guests since her passing a handful of years ago.

"So..." Tom said. "About the cleaning service?"

Logan's throat constricted. "Let me think about it." To his surprise, Tom let it drop.

"The call I took was something I need to respond to. It's not an emergency and it's close by, but I still better scoot."

"Thanks for everything." Logan shook his friend's hand, each clapping the other on the back.

"You should go for a ride," Tom suggested.

"Now?"

"You can't do anymore crime-scene-wise. Take a ride, clear your head. You'll work the case stronger that way."

He'd argue his head was already clear, but that would be a lie. It was as muddled as tar. "All right," he said. "That's not a bad idea." He had so many thoughts clamoring for purchase. Rides always straightened things out, and it was a gorgeous day for it—the sun high in the sky.

He turned to Em. "You up for one?"

"I've never been on a horse, but I'm always up for something new."

He loved he'd get to experience something with her for the first time. He wished he could experience everything new with her.

"You'll be a natural...as long as you don't ride Bathtub. She's a jealous girl."

"Hopefully, she won't mind me riding beside you."

"She better get used to it." Because that was where Emmy belonged.

J eff watched the sheriff leave and the other two remain. He'd think they were simply family in town for the upcoming funeral. Brought in to do a walk-through, see what was missing from the robbery. But the way the sheriff engaged them...the way they strode through the house. They weren't just looking the way family would. They were *examining* the crime scene.

Uneasiness raked through him, seizing his gut. Had they found something? Anything? Had Mary messed things up more than he'd realized? If she had, he'd kill her himself. Throttle the life from her.

He studied the pair as they moved about. They carried themselves like law enforcement, and they'd been meticulous with the crime scene—at least, it seemed that way from the glimpses he caught through the open window shades with his binoculars.

Had the sherriff called more investigators in to assist? If so, that meant he wasn't buying the setup—at least, not fully.

Jeff ground his teeth, his jaw locking.

They'd arranged it all so well. Made it appear like an open and shut case—a robbery gone wrong. But something wasn't right.

When the boss insisted that he stay behind to make sure the sheriff and his deputy bought it, he'd thought it a waste of time. Maybe the boss had been onto something after all. With the addition of the new pair, it wasn't looking good.

Thankfully, he'd stashed Mary and the truck. Gotten a new set of wheels for himself, made the stop he had to, and circled back. For all his boss knew, he'd remained in position the entire time as instructed.

He gave the pair one last look, his rapid pulse ticking in his neck. Something was definitely wrong.

Muttering a crass word under his breath, he rose up from lying belly-down in the dirt and set his binoculars aside. He was going to have to alert the boss and keep a keen eye on the pair. Far too much was at stake. If need be, they'd have to die, just like the old man who wouldn't let things rest.

TWELVE

"Hey, Logan," Em said, tugging his arm with a firm yet tender touch. "Let's talk for a minute before we ride," she said after Tom left and they were alone.

He never had the heart to say no to her, no matter how much he might want to—and he *did* want to at the moment because he knew what was coming. She was going to try to talk him out of cleaning the crime scene himself. He knew her motives were kind, that she wanted to spare him additional pain, but it was his grandpa, his home. His responsibility. Still, he'd let her say her piece. "All right," he said, following her to the porch. They'd left the front door open, hoping to air the space out now that the scene was cleared. Opening the windows would come next. It seemed the Santa Ana winds had a purpose other than tossing tumbleweeds around this year.

Em sat in a rocking chair and patted the one next to her.

He sank into it, adrenaline burning out.

The wind kicked up, clanging the cowbell overhead. The sound reverberated in his chest.

Em reached over and clasped his hand. "I agree with Tom about calling in a cleaning service." She tilted her head in that sweet, soft way of hers. "Don't put yourself through that. I didn't know your grandpa, but I can't imagine any grandpa wanting his grandson cleaning up...the scene," she said.

He inhaled and released it slowly, fighting off tears. He wouldn't cry. Not in front of her. Not at all. He was a man, and he'd take this on the chin. "I don't want..."

"Don't want what?" she asked, her voice full of compassion.

If he told her, she'd probably think he was being ridiculous. Maybe he was...

She rubbed his hand, her skin warm across his chilled fingers. "What is it?"

"I..." He cleared his throat. "I don't want them sterilizing Colt away." He dipped his head. "I don't mean the blood. I mean *him*—his smell of sunflower seeds and hay, the last things he touched that aren't covered in his blood." Who knew how much they'd eliminate, how far the cleaning would go.

At the very thought of it, he broke. Tears tumbled down his cheeks.

Em moved to kneel in front of him, her hands atop of his clutched ones. "Oh, Logan. I'm so sorry." She slid her right hand up to cup his cheek, and he leaned into her touch.

How could someone treat Colt—the best man he knew—like he didn't matter? Snuffing his life out then stealing from his person while he lay suffering and dying...who could be so callous and cruel?

"Honey," Em said, her hand caressing his face, her touch soft and warm.

She rose on her knees, her face nearly level with his.

His gaze fixed on the ground. He couldn't look at her. Embarrassment rushed through him at breaking down in front of her. But she'd have none of it. Gently yet firmly, she tipped his chin up, forcing him to look at her. She cupped both his cheeks, caressing them in soothing strokes.

He blinked through the tears. "He was such a good man," he said, his voice barely audible to his own ears. "The best man I kno—knew."

"You're a good man." She brushed the tears away as fast as they fell.

He shook his head. She wouldn't say that if she knew what he'd done. Once he told her, she'd never look at him the same again.

"Yes," she said, scooting closer so she was flush against his knees. "You are." She strained forward, placing a kiss on his right cheek.

He stilled at her touch. She'd never kissed him before, innocent though it was.

She blinked, then pressed a kiss to his forehead, stroking away the last of his tears.

He closed his eyes, remaining fixed in place, praying she wouldn't pull back.

"Such a good man," she whispered, kissing one closed lid and then the other.

"Em..." He breathed her name, cupping her face in his hands, her skin soft and supple beneath his touch.

Her breath caught, but she didn't pull away. Heaven help him, she leaned into his hold.

He lowered a hand to the small of her back and gently tugged her to him, needing to feel her close.

"Logan." His name came out a breathless whisper.

He clutched her tighter. He hovered his lips over hers, brushing a feather-light kiss across them.

She held still, warm in his embrace.

He pressed a whisper of a kiss across her lips, his hands

trembling. This was the woman he loved—the first and only one. Taking his time, he eased into a full kiss, pressing his lips deeply to hers. He feared with all that was within him she'd pull away, but she hesitantly, then tenderly returned the kiss—and he was lost.

THIRTEEN

Her lips tingling, her head swirling, she finally pulled back. Logan had *kissed* her. And she'd kissed him back, their lips melding. But she...*they*...

She took a steadying breath. She couldn't think straight.

"Em," he whispered, one of his hands still cupping her cheek, the other splayed across her back.

"We..." she started to say, but he interrupted.

"Please don't say we shouldn't have." The raw pleading in his voice made her breath catch. Had the kiss meant as much to him as it had to her? Or was he just emotional from the anguish of the day?

The sound of an engine roared in the distance.

She turned to look, waiting for the vehicle to come over the rise.

Logan released his hold on her, and the warmth left her body despite the heat of the day.

"We're continuing this later," he said matter-of-factly.

This? Did he mean the conversation...or the kiss? Heat flushed her cheeks. *Keep it together, Em.*

A smile tugged at the corner of his mouth—a mouth that had been on hers. Her limbs tingled.

He gave her hand a squeeze, a mixture of love and pain dancing in his weary eyes.

Tom's Tahoe came over the rise.

"I'd better go see what's up," he said, releasing her hand with clear reluctance.

She swallowed. She'd longed for the kiss. She'd spent over a year waiting, hoping.

But he was heartbroken, and while she wanted to provide as much comfort to him as possible, she didn't want comfort being the sole reason he kissed her.

Tom pulled to a stop, cut the ignition, and opened his door.

"That was fast," Logan said as Tom stepped from the vehicle.

"It went quick and smooth," he said.

"So, what's up?"

"We found the pawn shop," Tom said, a tinge of excitement in his tone.

Excitement, at least a hint of it, always filled her too when a lead opened up.

"Are you kidding?" Logan said. "That didn't take long." He looked over his shoulder at her as she strode to join them.

"We got lucky."

"So where'd she stop? What direction is she headed?" the words tumbled out in Logan's hope-filled voice.

It was the first time she'd heard him sound hopeful since Tom's fateful call. Hopeful for justice. She'd heard it before when they were getting close on a case.

Tom tipped his Stetson an inch higher so she could see his eyes. "At Sam's Treasures."

"Sam's Treasures?" Logan's brow furrowed. "As in, Sam Patterson's pawn shop?"

"Yep," Tom said. "Should we take a ride?" He moved to open the rear door for Emmy.

"Thank you." She smiled, climbing in.

Tom gestured to the passenger door, and Logan got in.

Logan buckled his seatbelt and looked over at Tom as he settled into the driver's seat. "Isn't Sam's shop west...and south of here?"

"Yeah. Weird, right?" Tom started the ignition.

Em clicked her seatbelt in place as the engine roared to life. "Why is that weird?"

"Sam's shop is in San Manuel." Tom pulled out of the driveway. "It's only a four-hour drive away. She could have made it much farther before he opened in the morning. When Mable relayed Sam's call, she said he noted that the ring had been pawned within minutes of opening up." He tore down the long drive leading out to the winding road. "So why'd she wait the night to hit Sam's shop? There are certainly more pawn shops down the road."

"She probably needed the money to get any further," Logan said. "And, San Manuel is a small town. She probably figured it was off the radar."

"True." Tom tapped the wheel. "It just makes more sense to hit a big city where you can disappear in the crowded population—or head for the border, for that matter. If there was enough gas in the tank to get her to San Manuel, then she could have gotten out of the States. It's less than four hours to the Mexican border in El Paso."

"But a female entering Mexico alone...that's super dangerous nowadays," Em said. A year or two back, she'd caught a movie on Netflix called *Bordertown*. It showcased the risks for a woman in Mexico with brutal and raw honesty. Since then, she'd kept up on the horrid news of women going missing and the awful sex trafficking that happened far too often in that area.

"It's certainly dangerous." Tom turned south on U.S. Route 180. "So is getting caught for murdering a man."

"True." She sat back against the seat.

"I think you both are right," Logan said.

"Huh?" Tom glanced over at him, then back to the paved road ahead.

"I think she—did you say she went by Mary?" Logan asked Tom.

He nodded. "No telling if that's her real name, of course."

"Let's just go with Mary for now. I think Mary knows the area and is trying to stay off grid. From San Manuel, she could go south to Tucson or north to Phoenix and get lost in either place."

Tom flipped on his blinker, shifting into the fast lane. "I'll get on the line with my fellow officers in Tucson and Phoenix. Let them know she could be headed their direction."

"But what I really want to know is where Mary hid out for the night." Em tapped her foot on the floorboard, adrenaline pumping through her veins. It always did when she was on a hunt.

"Good question." Tom angled his head. "Maybe you're right, and she knows someone in the area."

"Maybe that someone was the owner of the shoe print, if it turns out not to be Mary's."

Logan shifted to look back at her. "Good thought."

"I'm not saying it didn't belong to her, just that we shouldn't rule out other possibilities."

"Absolutely agree," Tom said. "But with the timing of the barricades and the drive to San Manuel..." he said, clearly thinking out loud. "She would have had to leave before they went up. So if she knows someone in the area, they either live outside of the barricaded zone we put up, or they went with her."

"Great point," Logan said, "but I'm still curious where she or possibly *they* spent the night."

"There are a ton of off-the-road motels from here to San Manuel she could have easily bunked up at," Tom said. "Some nice. Some on the very sleazy side."

"Lovely." Em sighed. No doubt they'd end up canvassing them all, but whatever it took to bring Colt's killer to justice. How anyone could murder an elderly man so brutally anchored in her mind and refused to let go.

T he patrol vehicle left, the two newcomers riding with the sheriff. They were definitely trouble. He'd done his part thus far and relayed the information to his boss. Now he'd wait to see what Keller discovered about the pair. If it turned out the two were a threat to their enterprise, he'd have no choice but to take them out. He toyed with the idea of doing it now—just getting it over with—but better not to jump the gun. He'd wait on Keller's instructions. His boss was never slow to act if action was required. In the meantime, he'd follow them. See where they were headed. He'd been too far away to hear their words, but given the sheriff had picked them up, it probably had to do with the case.

Tracking back to the car, Jeff climbed in and took the shortcut over to the main road. The ranch driveway was long, so he'd have to time it just right to come out behind them—close enough to follow but far enough back not to be seen.

FOURTEEN

J eff followed the sheriff's SUV from a solid distance away. On a two-lane road in the middle of nowhere USA, there wasn't a way to blend into traffic with only a few cars on the highway.

The sheriff and the pair might be smart, but he was smarter. Keller thought him just a fool to boss around and do his dirty work, but he knew how to outplay the doc. Keller didn't own him like he thought he did.

Continuing south on Route 180, he relaxed against the seat, deciding to turn on some music. They were probably just headed for Silver City. He had nothing to worry about. It was the opposite direction of Mary.

He turned the radio dial. Nothing but static, but what had he expected in the barren land? He tried his music streaming app, but couldn't get it to work. He slammed his phone down on the passenger seat. Of course, there'd be no cell service either.

He released a heavy exhale, frustration raking through him. This was most likely a waste of his time, but he needed to see where they went. What they were up to. They clearly thought they had something.

He straightened as they took 78 West. His grip on the steering wheel tightened, blood draining from his clamped fingers. They couldn't be...

"What's up?" Em said, when she saw Logan looking back from the front passenger seat.

"There's this car." The moment he said it, the car eased back, letting the minivan it'd passed just two miles back pass it.

"You think we have a tail?" Tom asked. "The white car?"

"Yeah. I didn't think much of it while we were on 180. Pretty much all cars on it are headed for Silver City. But when it crossed over the New Mexico–Arizona line, it—"

"—pricked your Spidey sense," Em said with a smile.

He remembered her learning the phrase from a friend she had back East, but in this case, it readily applied. Something about the car stuck with him. "Yeah," he said, bracing his hand on the seatback as he shifted to keep a better eye on the car. "You have a pair of binoculars in here? I'd like to try and make out if it's a woman or a man driving. I can't tell from this distance."

"Binoculars in the glovebox," Tom said, and Logan grabbed them. "I'll ease back, see if we can get the minivan to pass us."

"Good idea."

Tom took his foot off the gas, slowing down gradually.

"Come on," Logan said, irritation sparking his leg into a bounce. "Just pass us," he grunted at the minivan.

Tom slowed his speed more.

Logan looked at the road ahead and then back at the minivan blocking their view of the white car. The curve up ahead would give him a clear view of the cars rounding it. "You can't stay hidden for long," he said. But if the car was following them—why? And more importantly, who? Was it Colt's killer trying to keep an eye on them, on their investigation? His stomach flipped. Was she that close?

Tom eased around the curve. The white car came into view, but it'd drawn back even more—out of the range where Logan could make a definitive call on the sex of the driver.

"Shoot," he said, his leg bouncing harder.

"Too far back?" Em asked.

"Yes, but if I had to take a guess, I'd say it's a man. The overall frame suits a man better." He'd caught sight of the front plate—the decorative one. Why couldn't New Mexico require actual front license plates? All he could see was the old style, a bright yellow plate with a red symbol. At least it was recognizable from a solid distance, but that did them no good.

"We're getting off at the junction in Three Way. Let's see if he follows onto Route 191."

"Good idea," Logan said, drumming his fingers on the back of his seat, his body still turned to face the rear windshield. *Come on.* He tried to will the car to follow them as Tom moved through Three Way, taking 191 South.

The white car took the junction to SR 78.

Logan shifted back around. "I guess not," he said.

"It may have just been someone headed the same way for a while," Em said. "Though you're hardly ever wrong about stuff like this."

His gut said he was right.

J eff banged the wheel of the stolen sedan. They'd made him. But it didn't matter. He knew exactly where they were headed. *Sam's Treasures.* His gut twisted. They'd found it far too fast for his liking. But in the end, it really made no difference. No way they could ID him. He'd been too careful.

Afterward, they'd no doubt waste their time searching for Mary in nearby Tucson or possibly head up to Phoenix. They'd assume she'd gone to get lost in the crowd of one of the bigger cities. It was what made sense. They'd never figure she'd circle back, because it made zero sense—which was exactly why it was the right move.

Once he was far enough up the road, he turned around, heading back for the junction in Three Way. He'd find a new car. There had to be one unattended at a gas station or whatever was in that nothing of a town. Then he'd head for Sam's, would watch them come out of the pawn shop through his long-range binoculars. See how they looked. How confident they appeared. Most importantly, he'd make sure they headed in the wrong direction. Then he'd be golden.

FIFTEEN

Logan's neck still prickled as he held the door of Sam's Treasures open for Em. She stepped inside, then he and Tom followed. Everything inside him still said they'd been followed, at least until Three Way, Arizona. The car may have gone a different way at the junction, but that didn't rule out the possibility they'd been tailed until that point. His gut remained uneasy, not helped by the quick fast-food lunch they'd gotten at a drive-through on the way.

He looked around, shifting his focus to what was tangibly before him. The shop hadn't changed much from when Old Leroy owned it. Growing up, visiting pawn shops with Tom had been an adventure. It had been fun to go through buckles rodeo guys had pawned and random treasures from older folks looking to clear out their houses. They'd found some really cool stuff, like an old Texas Ranger's badge. Why anyone would pawn something like that baffled him at the time, but now that he was older and more experienced, he knew that people usually pawned things either when desperate for cash or trying to get rid of an old memory.

"Hey, Logan," Sam said, stepping around the counter. "Is that you?"

"Hey, man." He clasped Sam's hand. "It's been a while." Sam looked the same except for a few gray streaks in his dark hair.

"I'd say a decade at least."

"Yeah, I'd say that's about right." He'd left for college in South Carolina at eighteen, and though he'd been back home often, he hadn't visited pawn shops during those visits like he and Tom used to as kids. But then, Sam hadn't owned a pawn shop all those years ago. He'd been the high school baseball coach—*his* old coach.

"So you bought Leroy's place?" he said.

"Yeah." Sam smiled. "Rachel wanted to be closer to her family, with the kids and all."

"How is your wife?"

"Doing great, thanks." Sam pulled a wrapped item from underneath the counter and laid it atop the glass display case. "I assume you're here for this." He pulled back the tan cloth. In the center lay Mee-Maw's wedding ring—a ruby instead of a diamond set in the center with small diamonds surrounding it. Colt went big or broke.

"This is what you're looking for, right?" Sam asked.

"Yes," Logan said. "Thank you for holding onto it." Colt always said he could give it to his own wife when the time came. He never thought it would, but... He looked over at Em, and the ache in him grew.

"No need to thank me." Sam braced his hands on the glass counter of the display case." I'm just sorry I didn't realize who it belonged to when the guy came in."

"A guy?" Em frowned.

"Yeah. A dude came in to pawn it."

"Mable didn't mention that," Tom said, rocking back on his heels.

"That was probably my fault," Sam said. "I just said the ring had been pawned here."

"No worries," Tom said. "Tell us more about the guy."

"He said he'd bought the ring for his girlfriend, but they split, so he wanted the cash instead. You'd be surprised how many times that happens around here," Sam said.

Logan looked at Em and then Tom. They were all thinking the same thing. The possibility of there being a mystery man had just increased.

"I'm guessing a woman didn't accompany him in?" Em asked the next question on Logan's mind.

"Nope." Sam shook his head.

"By any chance, did you see one waiting outside?" Tom asked.

"Can't say I did, but I wasn't looking for one," Sam said. "It was before I saw the sketch of the lady you sent over along with the list of items you were looking for."

Logan stiffened. Whatever she was, she wasn't a lady.

Sam shook his head. "I can't believe Colt's gone." He looked to Logan, compassion in his brown eyes. "My deepest sympathies."

"Thanks." Logan dipped his chin.

"What about the other items that were taken?" Tom asked. "I take it the guy didn't bring them in?"

"Nope. Just the ring. Colt's revolver, I would have recognized straight away. It's legendary."

Logan shucked his hands in his pockets. "Legendary" was how he'd describe the man himself. His history had been full of escapades that kept Logan glued to his grandpa's stories as a kid.

Sam grabbed the copy of the woman's sketch that had been

sent over. "She looks pretty rough," he said. "You thinking drugs?"

"That's our supposition," Tom said.

"I'm glad you've got a sketch to go on. Surely, someone will see her at some point."

"If she hasn't disguised herself," Em said.

"Yeah..." Sam leaned on the counter, his forearms resting atop the glass. "But those eyes are pretty memorable."

"Yes," Tom agreed. "Thankfully, Denton got a decent look at her."

"So...Denton." Sam tapped the sketch lying on the counter beside him. "I remember Denton well." He looked to Logan.

Adrenaline burned through his arms as his mind cast back to those days. As their coach, Sam had witnessed Denton's bullying of Logan firsthand. While Sam kiboshed it on the field and in the locker rooms, he couldn't stop it off school property. But he'd practically cheered the day Logan finally stood up to Denton. It was the day that had changed everything between them.

"I'm sorry I didn't see the woman," Sam said, shifting the conversation back on topic. "She should be behind bars." He pinned the sketch of her on the bulletin board behind the counter. "But I've got the footage of the guy if you'd like to see it."

"Absolutely," Tom said.

Logan looked down at Mee-Maw's ring still lying on the counter, then at Tom.

"Can I take the ring back home?" he asked.

"I'd like to run it for prints," Tom said, "but we can do that easily enough at the station. No need to send it to the lab."

"Thanks," Logan said, knowing Tom would process it personally to get it back to him all the sooner.

"Uh..." Sam rubbed the back of his neck. "That might be a problem."

Logan frowned. "I don't understand."

"When rings come in, they go in the deep cleaner, "Sam said, "and then I shine them with the Dremel. Any prints would have been wiped out. Sorry, guys. I had no idea."

"No way you could have known," Tom said.

"If only I'd checked my email first, but the guy walked in about two minutes after I opened."

"Did you see his car in the parking lot?" Tom asked, looking back at the glass entrance door.

"No. He must have pulled into one of the side slots."

"After we see the footage, let's print a screenshot of him, and I'll get it sent out to law enforcement agencies."

"Unfortunately, I don't think you're going to have much to send."

SIXTEEN

Sam was one of those early risers and opened the shop at seven a.m. The man had entered at three minutes after. He'd worn a Yankee's hat under his hoodie—and they only knew that much because of Sam, since the cap wasn't visible on the video footage given the way he'd kept his head down. In the end, other than his race, basic build, and choice of clothes, they had nothing to go on.

"It's disappointing that we don't have any direct leads on Mary," Logan said as they climbed back in Tom's patrol SUV at the San Manuel bus station. "It's so frustrating that no one has seen her, but, for me at least, it only increases my interest in our mystery man."

"Agreed," Tom said, pulling back onto the main road leading out of San Manuel. After canvassing the town well into the evening and finding no leads, they were headed back for Cauldron Creek.

"It fits with no one recognizing Mary at the bus station," Em said, stretching out. "She had to find another way here. The most likely option is our mystery man helped her out."

"So, you're thinking she ditched the truck?" Logan asked, stretching his arms out.

"Yes." She crossed her legs, trying to not pay attention to how tired they were. How tired *she* was. She hadn't slept since the night before they flew to New Mexico. And with it now nearly eight o'clock, they wouldn't be getting back to Cauldron Creek before midnight. She might find herself dozing off during the drive. "My guess is that she dumped Colt's truck as fast as she could, and if she didn't have someone helping her with a ride already, then she found someone."

"So you think she hitched a ride," Tom said.

"Potentially," Em said. "These are all just options. Logan and I like to run as many possible ones as we can, even if they aren't probable."

"Okay. Let's run with the theory of her hitching a ride," Tom said, looking in the rearview mirror at Em. He was clearly enjoying the exchange of ideas. "Then what?"

"She talked the man who entered Sam's shop into hocking the ring." Em shifted again, trying to find a comfy position for the four-hour ride back. "I'm guessing, if that's the case, she'd probably offered to split the cash he got for it."

"Good theory," Logan said. "But how would she know that she could trust the guy to bring half back to her?"

"Good question," she said, shrugging a shoulder. The possibilities ran through her mind as they drove through the darkness—the moon illuminating the trees standing like stick figures along the road. "Maybe she was offering him something other than money as payment," she said, not wanting to think that one through any further. "Or maybe she was watching close by."

"Sam said he never saw the car the guy drove. Maybe she was waiting for the guy in it," Logan said, looking over his shoulder at her. Did he yearn for them to be alone together as much as she did? And yet, the idea scared her. The kiss had suddenly made everything so real, so fast. It was what she wanted, but was it what he truly wanted, too?

"Excellent point," Tom said. "She could have very well been waiting in the car. The big question is, where did she, or *they,* head after Sam's?"

There were so many possibilities before them. Too many. They needed something substantial. Tangible.

L ogan waved bye to Tom as he drove away, thankful to be back at the ranch. He glanced at Em. She was tired, and they were both hungry—but after two meals of fast food eaten on the go, they'd refused Tom's offer of another drive-through on the way back.

"Let's get to Aunt Rae's, and I'll make us something to eat."

She nodded and took hold of his hand as they made their way to the big red barn.

"Here we are," he said.

Em's nose crinkled. "We're sleeping in a barn?"

He smiled. "You'll see." He opened the narrow sliding door, and she followed him into the dark building. "Stand still until I get the lights," he said.

The lights flicked on, and Em's eyes grew wide.

"What do you think of Aunt Rae's place?" he asked.

Em stepped further inside the totally renovated barn.

To him, it still held the charm of a barn but with all the comforts of a cozy home.

"I love it." She smiled. "Such a cool place." She cast her gaze up to what had originally been a hayloft. "I adore the loft."

He followed her gaze to the sitting area visible through the white, spindle railing, and smiled. "Tom and I used to make forts up there, hanging sheets and blankets across the open area." Good memories flooded his mind. "Colt built in some secret spots when he remodeled the barn for Aunt Rae. He'd leave coded messages for us, and we'd spend the night in our fort, flashlights on, trying to crack the codes."

"That's so cool. Think anything's still in the hiding spots?"

"Good question. I can check in the morning." There'd been a message in the cash box and an old treasure in the bunkhouse —why not a leftover message in Aunt Rae's?

She tilted her head in that set way of hers. "You know I won't settle until you check. You do that, and I'll make us something to eat...that is, if there's food here.

"I got a text from Bucky. He dropped off meals from nearly everyone in town while we were in San Manuel."

"That's so sweet. Tom said that would happen."

"Yeah. There's a lot to be said for small towns." Not that Wilmington, NC, was huge by any means, but with over a hundred thousand people compared to the two hundred and three in Cauldron Creek, there was a big difference.

"I'll poke my head in the fridge and see what I can heat up." She strode across the open living space for the galley-style kitchen.

"I can do that," he said. "It's been a long day—long forty-eight hours, really, since either of us has slept."

"I'm fine," she said, rummaging through the fridge. "Now shoo. I'm too curious about those hiding spots to wait until morning."

"Okay." He chuckled. When Em set her mind to something... Besides, it bought him a little more time before the talk he knew they needed to have, now that they'd kissed. She deserved to know about his past before things went any further between them. It could wait until morning, probably *should* wait until morning, so she could get some rest that was well overdue.

She looked up at him with an aluminum pan in hand. "Homemade mac and cheese?" she asked. "The instructions on it say thirty minutes to heat up, not bad."

"Sounds good."

She set to work on popping it into the oven. "Shoo already," she said, flicking her hand at him.

"Yes, ma'am." He held up his hands. "Going, but I doubt there'll be anything here. Colt kept his reminders in the house. The one in the bunkhouse was left over from years ago."

"So maybe something will be left over here, too. I'd love to see."

"All right," The woman was so stubborn. If he didn't look, she'd go running through the place herself. At least this way, she could sit on the couch while the mac and cheese heated up and kick her feet on the ottoman, getting as comfortable as she could in her skirt and blouse. He'd suggest that she get changed, but he doubted she had relaxation clothes or jeans in her go-bag. In fact, he'd never seen her in jeans. He really needed to get the woman some comfier clothes to rest in.

Curiosity nipped at him as he moved for Colt's first hiding spot—the one in the kitchen. Reaching under the cupboard on the far right, he pulled out the small drawer hidden underneath and emerged with another roll of paper like they'd found with Colt's wad of cash. He held it up so Em could see.

"Fun!" Her we're-on-the-hunt smile popped up, despite the tiredness in her eyes.

He shook his head. She was a mess. A beautiful mess. But he needed to do this fast so she would eat when dinner was ready and then head to bed. With two bedrooms, they'd each have a room tonight, which—he stretched, his body aching—suited him far better than the sofa would.

"Open it," she said, leaning over the sofa arm.

"Okay," he said, sitting down beside her.

He unraveled the tightly rolled piece of paper and furrowed his brow. It was as recent as the one in the cash box—Colt's scrawl getting shakier over the years, making the age of the messages easy to figure out. This message had three rows of numbers. His mind returned to memories of Colt and the messages they shared. The suffocating weight of loss bore down on him once more.

Em narrowed her eyes and reached over to place a hand on his knee.

How could her simple touch reassure him so much?

"You okay?" she asked.

"Yeah." He cleared his throat, turning his attention back to Colt's note.

She leaned closer, sidling up beside him. Her warmth brought him an unspoken measure of peace.

"What does the message say?" she asked, her eyes alight with intrigue.

"Take a look." He handed it to her.

"I'll go to the next spot while you play with what it might mean."

"Okay." She gave a soft smile, then directed her attention on the puzzle, that adorable inquisitive gleam in her eye as she studied it.

Heading into the bathroom on the lower level, he knelt by the toilet pedestal. Of all the places to hide a message, this was his least favorite to check, but back in the day, this was where Colt always hid the best messages. He reached where the pedestal met the base of the sink bowl and ran his fingers along the smooth porcelain until he felt the rolled-up paper. Bingo! He pulled it out and unraveled it. Three rows of numbers this time. Each row held an equal number of numerals, but these had dashes throughout each row—two numbers then a dash, four more and a dash, then two more and a final dash. There was a row of what looked like dates by them. This message was scrawled in the same messy handwriting, so it'd been penned within the last few months. *What on earth was his grandpa up to?*

"Anything?" Em called from the living room.

"Yep." He got to his feet and tucked the note in his pocket. "I'll check the last hiding spot, then come show you."

"Okay." Excitement rang in her voice, and he saw the same smile on her face as he strode back by the couch and moved toward the original barn ladder leading up to the loft.

Reaching the top, he stepped onto the carpeted seating area. A bedroom branched off on either side of the loft space—an addition his grandpa and Bucky had built for Aunt Rae when they'd fully renovated the barn for her to live in after Uncle Guy passed. Logan paused in the loft area overlooking the lower floor of the barn. His gaze fixed on Em and a smile tugged at his lips. Only she could make him smile under such heart-wrenching circumstances.

The smile certainly didn't erase the pain. Instead, it buffered it some as God hid him in the shelter of His wings.

"Anything?" Em called up.

"Checking now." Shaking off the thoughts racing through his mind, he entered the guest bedroom to the right of the sitting area and flicked on the light. He strode to the dresser and reached behind it to the secret panel that looked innocuous —like an access panel for wiring or to reach an air vent. Definitely Colt's coolest hiding spot. He loved the lengths Colt had gone to for their coded message games. They had brought him out of a dark, dark place.

Logan opened the panel and reached inside. Feeling around with his hand, he was about to give up when his fingers landed on something. He pulled out the roll of tightly wound paper, fastened in place with a small, looped rubber band.

It was fun finding messages, but what on earth was Colt doing still hiding codes in the walls? He could see the sense in using the hiding spot in the main house as Colt had taken to leaving important messages in there for himself, but all the way at Aunt Rae's? It didn't make much sense. Tucking the rolled-up paper in his pants pocket where the one from the bathroom already resided, he hurried down to Em.

"Find another one?" she asked, sitting up straighter, almost perched to receive the news.

He sat down beside her, pulled the two rolls out of his pocket, and handed her one.

Removing the rubber band, she flattened it on the coffee table in front of them. She frowned at the numbers. "What do you think it means? I mean what kind of codes did you use to leave each other?"

"Ciphers or number puzzles, but only this one..." he said, unraveling the last roll he'd taken from the guest room, "...looks like one of our Ottendorf ciphers. The others must be number puzzles, but they look different than the ones we used to do."

"In what sense?"

"We always did number fill-in or slide-and-merge number puzzles. These just look like regular lines of numbers, but they must mean more, or Colt wouldn't have bothered tucking them in the hiding spots. I just don't understand why he'd hide them all the way here rather than in the main house."

"Hmm." Em leaned forward, propping her elbows on her thighs. "Maybe if you decode the cipher, it'll point us in the right direction for solving the other puzzles. What cipher key do you think he used?"

"He always used his Louis L'Amour novels."

"Okay." She scanned Aunt Rae's bookshelves.

"They're not here," he said. "They're in the main house."

"Ah. Because you never keep the cipher and the key together," she said.

That was the girl he loved—so smart and methodical.

"Okay. Let's play with the other two," she said, as the oven timer went off.

"I'll grab the food," Logan said, moving for the galley kitchen. Slipping on a pair of oven mitts from the side drawer, he opened the oven. A wave of heat washed over him, and he pulled the steaming pan out, setting it on top of the stove before turning off the oven. "We're going to need to let that cool a while."

"Good," she said. "That'll give us time to look at the other two messages."

"You're already addicted." He chuckled, a little surprised that she had managed to make him chuckle at all. Even if it was a fleeting moment of happiness, it brought a small measure of joy to his cracked soul.

Setting the cipher message aside for now, Em laid the other two messages out on the coffee table, smoothing her hand across them to flatten them out.

Logan leaned forward, studying the numbers. "The ones with the dashes...if the dashes were shifted around... You have a pencil or pen in your purse?" he asked.

"Of course." She retrieved her bag off the end table. "Which would you prefer?"

"A pencil would be great. Thanks," he said as she handed it to him. "Oh, wait. I need paper."

She reached back in her bag and pulled out a small, flip notebook.

At this point, he figured she had anything he could ask for in there.

He set the notebook open on the coffee table, then he bent over and started rearranging the dashes.

Em's brows arched when he hit it. "Phone numbers?"

"Yep. And then dates."

"So most likely the dates he made the calls," she said.

Why on earth had Colt been hiding phone numbers at Aunt Rae's place?

Em pulled out her cell. "Let's give them a dial."

He nodded. "You take the first, I'll take the second, and whoever finishes first can take the third."

"Deal," she said, dialing before he could even pull his phone from his trousers.

Jeff bounced his leg, waiting for the boss to answer. He'd told Keller something was up with the pair. Now he waited to see what his boss had discovered. Keller did the digging while he did the messy jobs. But for how civilized Keller liked to act, Jeff knew the truth of his boss's depravity and just how low he'd sink when necessary.

Turning his back against the wind, he momentarily took his eyes off the barn as ideas for scaring them off raced through his mind. At the very least, they needed to be kept from continuing their investigation—but watching the pair thus far, he doubted they'd back down easily.

Keller had insisted he keep an eye on the couple, but the longer he was away from Mary, the itchier he grew.

Finally, Keller answered. "It's about time you called."

It was about time he answered. "What did you find out?"

"The man is the grandson, as I assumed, but you were right to think there's something more there. He and the woman are special agents."

Jeff stiffened. "Special agents? With the feds?"

"Not exactly. They're both with the Coast Guard Investigative Service."

Jeff raked a hand through his spiky hair, the gelled tips hard to the touch. "Then why are they investigating here? This has nothing to do with the Coast Guard."

"Investigating is what investigators do. Given the fact that the old man was Agent Perry's grandpa, I'm sure he's fully bent on solving this case, which we can't allow to happen. We have too much at stake. Do you understand me?"

Jeff gripped the phone tighter. Now Keller wanted him taking out special agents? He didn't mind the loss of life. What he did mind was going to prison for murdering federal agents.

"Do you *understand* me?" Keller repeated, his words clipped and cutting. "It's too dangerous leaving them alive. With their background and training, they could foul everything up. You need to take them out now! You hear me?"

Jeff swallowed hard. "I hear you."

"Then what's the hesitation? You don't want to end up like Layton, do you?"

The man he'd replaced. The man Keller had killed and buried in a dry bed along the Rio Grande.

"No," he bit out.

"Good. Make it look like an accident. Two murdered agents would draw far too much attention."

"Then maybe we should leave them alive."

"And give them time to figure things out? Don't be stupid. We need to nip their investigation in the bud. As long as the accident is well-staged, no one will think any more of it."

Jeff forced back his scoff. Yeah, because that had worked so well with staging the old man's murder as a robbery.

"Are we clear?" Keller said, his tone hard and unyielding.

"Fine, but my price just went up."

"Don't mess with me. You're getting paid plenty already. Besides, do I need to remind you what I'm capable of if you disobey my orders?" A harsh edge, one that sliced straight through a man, seethed in Keller's voice.

He knew what Keller was capable of. But did Keller know what *he* was capable of? He played this sick game because it paid well, but there was only so far he'd go.

"Jeff!" Keller hollered.

Jeff didn't say a word as he ran the scenarios through his mind. Maybe he could turn the tables. Put Keller in the hot seat. Take their earnings and disappear, letting Keller rot in jail.

"Trust me," Keller said, malice thick in his voice. "You don't want me coming out there to take care of things myself. Do we have an understanding?"

"I'll see what I can do." He'd think long and hard, and then he'd decide what was best for *him*, whether that meant falling in line with Keller or not.

"Don't see," Keller bit out. "Do it."

"And my monetary compensation for taking a higher risk?" he said, circling back to his request.

"I'll be sure you're properly compensated."

"Now," Jeff said.

"Excuse me?"

"Send along a money order, and then I'll take care of the pair."

"And how much do you expect this bonus fee to be?"

"Ten grand."

"You're out of your mind."

"Then come kill them yourself." He hung up, but waited, counting to himself.

One. Two. Three.

His cell rang. There it was.

"We have a deal," Keller said. "Now kill them!"

SEVENTEEN

Logan dialed the number, then paced the area rug while it rang.

"Albuquerque General," a woman answered.

Logan frowned. "Albuquerque General?"

"Yes, sir. How can I direct your call?"

"I'm sorry. I don't know, exactly," he said. "I'll call back when I do. But thank you for your time." He turned back to find Em holding up one finger. She was already on her second call.

He sat back down beside her and waited, but she didn't talk, just frowned.

"What's up?" he asked when she hung up.

"It was a Medicare office. I got a recording, of course," she said.

Logan looked at his watch. 0045. They had to wrap this up. The talk he needed to have with Em would have to wait until the morning. But at least they'd figured out where the numbers led, even if they had to wait until Monday to get ahold of the

Medicare office. "It's after midnight," he said. "We need to eat and get to sleep."

She nodded. "But don't you want to know about the first number I dialed?" she asked, as he moved for the mac and cheese resting atop the stove.

"Oh right. Of course." Pulling two plates from the open shelf mounted on the wall, he grabbed a serving spoon from the crock jar on the counter.

"Tucson Medical Supply Company," she said.

"Medical supply?" He frowned, scooping them each a decent serving of mac and cheese. "That's where Mee-Maw got her medical equipment. But since she's gone home to be with the Lord, I have no idea why Colt would be calling them. Even less clue why he'd hide the numbers here." He grabbed two forks and a pile of napkins and carried them over to the coffee table.

"Here you go," he said, setting her plate in front of her and handing her a fork.

"Thanks," she said. "Naturally, given the late hour, I got a recording. It said they're closed on Sundays, so we'll have to wait until Monday morning to reach back out." She speared the mac and cheese with her fork. "What about your call?" she asked, before popping the bite in her mouth.

"One of the hospitals in Albuquerque," he said, laying the napkin across his lap.

"So it's clearly something medical Colt was dealing with."

Logan exhaled. "I'd wager you're right. I hate that we have to wait until Monday to figure out what he was calling about. And even when we get ahold of someone, it might be a dead end if no one remembers speaking with him at the Medicare office or the medical supply store. The hospital is too large at this point to try and figure out why he called there. Regardless," he said, gesturing to the coded papers on the edge of the table, "the calls must have some special meaning, or why bother hiding and encoding the numbers?" They both ate in silence for the next few minutes, processing what they'd learned. When his plate was cleared, Logan stood and took it to the dishwasher. "For now, it's time for sleep."

"But the other puzzles?" she said.

So far, they'd only solved one.

"They can wait until morning. We need to sleep."

A half hour later, Logan lay in bed. Knowing Em was right across the loft filled him with both peace and trepidation. They'd been too tired for a serious relationship talk tonight. But come tomorrow morning, he had to tell her. They'd finally crossed the friendship barrier. Before things went any further, he needed to tell her the truth of who he was—the shame that defined him.

"Morning," Em said, climbing down the ladder.

"Perfect timing," he said, setting eggs, bacon, and toast on the dining table.

"I thought I smelled bacon...and coffee, hopefully?"

"Yes, ma'am," he said, pouring her a cup.

"I have to admit, I'm enjoying this service."

He smiled and took a seat. They'd eat, and then they'd talk.

Later on, they'd finish up with Colt's puzzles. He prayed Tom would call soon with a lead to go on—a sighting of Mary or the missing items—something, *anything* that would provide their next step.

Em took a sip of coffee and her gaze lifted up to Aunt Rae's sketches. "Wow. I was so tired last night...I didn't even notice the artwork. They're so lovely."

"They're Aunt Rae's," he said. "She's the one who taught me how to sketch."

"Oh cool," she said, as she buttered a slice of toast. "I'd love to see her sketches sometime."

He smiled. "You're looking at them."

She frowned. "Those don't look like sketches...more like watercolor paintings."

"Yeah, she worked with watercolor pencils."

"Pencils did that?"

"Yep." He looked at the beautiful sunset scene Aunt Rae had sketched from the porch of the main house. He remembered that day, standing beside her, opting to sketch with her charcoal instead.

Em tilted her head. "But you prefer charcoal? Or is that just due to job requirements?" she asked, before taking a bite of her toast.

"No. I always liked black and white." Right and wrong. Justice and injustice. Life had always been black and white to him until Em. She had a way of lighting the world up with color.

"Speaking of sketches..." she said.

"Yes?"

"The sketch you did of me..." Vulnerability shone in her eyes.

Em...vulnerable?

"Is that how you see me?" she asked, almost tentative. "Beautiful like that?"

"Absolutely." How could she think anything but? "You are breathtaking."

Surprise radiated in her beautiful eyes. "You think I'm breathtaking?"

He swept a stray lock of hair behind her ear, his finger

trailing down along her neck, feeling her pulse beating under it. "You're the most beautiful woman I've ever seen."

Her gaze dropped down. "I saw some of the women you went out with. They were gorgeous."

He tipped her chin up, gently forcing her to meet his gaze. He needed her to see the earnestness in his eyes. "They couldn't hold a candle to you. I only had eyes for you. Only *have* eyes for you."

She furrowed her brow. "Then why?"

"The serial dating?"

She nodded.

He took a stiff inhale, then released it. His turn to be vulnerable. "I didn't think you'd ever go for a guy like me...not the way I was back then." He ran his hand through her hair, his fingers splaying until he cradled the base of her neck tenderly. "You know I changed because of you. Became alive because of you."

"Me?" she squeaked.

"You know—" His voice cracked.

She scooted closer until their chairs knocked. "I know...?" she nudged.

"You're everything to me." He released a shaky exhale. He needed to tell her now. "But..."

Confusion marred her fair brow. "But?"

EIGHTEEN

L ogan sat back, the expression in his eyes flickering from love to shame.

"What happened?" she asked.

He narrowed his eyes. "Why do you think something happened?"

"Something must have happened to make you..."

He raked a hand through his hair, his shoulders taut. "Make me?"

"To haunt you," she said.

"You're entirely too perceptive."

He'd said it many times, but she couldn't help it. It was a gift God had blessed her with, though she didn't know if Logan viewed it as a gift right now.

"Let's go sit on the couch," he said, scooting back and offering his hand.

What on earth was he going to tell her? She took his hand, and they moved to the sofa.

"Okay..." He rubbed his thighs, then cleared his throat. "When I was five and my mom was expecting my baby brother,

I—" Pain etched his face, the flush of shame reddening his cheeks.

"You...?" she asked, reaching for his hands.

"Do you remember the big china cabinets or hutches people had in their dining rooms when we were growing up? You don't see them much anymore."

"The ones with a solid bottom with drawers while the top half had glass doors and shelves?" she asked. Her mom still had one in the dining room of her childhood home.

"Exactly," he said, clutching her hands.

"Yeah, I remember," she said. She edged towards him, closing the distance, unsure where this was going.

"I knew my dad kept his candy stash on top of the cabinet—and that day, I knew that he was going to be home soon, which meant that if I wanted to sneak one without getting caught, I had to hurry. I'd learned how to pull one of the dining chairs over. Then I'd open the glass doors and use the glass shelves inside to climb the rest of the way up." He swallowed hard. "Half-balancing on the top shelf, I'd hang on to the woodwork design at the top, then reach into the candy bowl." His voice cracked, and sorrow twisted her stomach, already imagining all the ways that this could go wrong.

"That day..." He looked down. "I lost my grip and knocked hard into the shelf, shattering it beneath me. Before I knew what was happening, I was falling, everything tumbling down with me. My mom..." The words choked in his throat, and he cleared it again. "...her belly round with my baby brother. She saw me and raced forward to try to get to me before I hit the floor."

Emmy's breath hitched. *Please, Father, don't let this be going where I think it is.*

"I crashed right into her." His voice shuddered, and she

gripped his hands as tight as she could, an ache burrowing in her gut.

"I knocked her to the ground, on top of all the broken glass." Weary tears beaded in his eyes.

The air knocked from her lungs.

"My dad came rushing in, screaming at me to get off my mom. Screaming, 'what have you done?'" Logan dipped his head, averting his eyes. "I didn't understand what the blood on my mom's dress meant. But I learned..." He swiped at his eyes with the back of his hand. "My baby brother died that day because of me."

***

L ogan's muscles coiled with tension as tears slipped from his eyes. He swiped them away with the back of his hand, hesitant to look at Emmy, to witness her reaction.

Her warm hand rested on his cheek, and she nudged his head up. "Look at me," she whispered.

The moment of truth. Bracing himself for disgust, he looked up...and found only love in her eyes. *Love?*

It was just how his mom had looked at him on that day—and every day after. She'd continued to tell him over and over that it'd been an accident and that it wasn't his fault. She'd kept saying that right up until the day his dad took him away and dumped him on Colt's doorstep.

"Is that why you came to live with Colt?" she asked.

He took a jagged inhale. "Yes. My dad brought me. Told Colt to take me."

She closed the tiny bit of space between them, her knees touching his, tears brimming in her eyes. "And your mom?"

"She sent letters. Said she'd come for me soon, but days turned to weeks, which turned to a year." His jaw tensed, and she caressed it. "One day, a letter came from my dad. Colt never let me see it, but he told me my mom had died in a car accident."

"Oh, honey." She kissed his forehead. "I'm so sorry."

"My dad came to town a few weeks after her death. I didn't know it at the time—Colt only told me later."

"Why did he come?"

"For the reading of the will. Colt said my dad was furious my mom had retained a lawyer behind his back in her '*pathetic hometown.*'"

"He sounds like a winner." She bit her lip. "Sorry."

"No. It's true. I've come to terms with him being a horrible person," Logan said. His father had made plenty of mistakes, but none could compare to what *he'd* done to his mom...to his baby brother. That was where the shame resided, gnawing in his gut, in his soul. "But..." he added, taking solace in this part. "The real kicker was my mom left everything to me for when I turned eighteen."

"Your trust fund?"

"Yeah." His team all knew he was a trust fund kid and didn't need to work. But Colt had raised him right—with a strong work ethic. That, combined with his drive for justice—for righting wrongs—meant that he could never just sit by and not do anything. "Colt and Mee-Maw owned some oil rights up in North Dakota," he continued. "They bought Mom a few shares when she was small..."

"And they hit oil?" Em guessed.

"Big time. She was rich, and Dad didn't even know it until she died and the will was read."

"Sounds like he got what he deserved."

"He did, but *I* didn't."

"Logan, you know it was an accident," Em said, echoing his mother's tender words. "You were just a little boy."

A little boy who had hurt his mommy, as his dad refused to let him forget.

Emmy's face softened even further. "Is that why you were so antagonistic about God for all those years?"

"I didn't see how a good God could let my brother die. Or why He wouldn't punish me for what I did."

"Logan, we live in a broken world," she said.

"Broken or not, I was bitter, angry...resentful. I lost my brother and my family that day. For the longest time, it was easier to blame God than to deal with the fact that I didn't deserve to be saved."

Her brows furrowed. "None of us deserve to be saved. That's why we all so desperately need Jesus. And you didn't deserve to be punished, either. It was an accident."

"That's what Noah said." His boss was equally his friend, and when he'd gone to him with questions about Jesus, Noah had been only too happy to chat over and over again.

"Because it's the truth," Em said.

"It took time, but I came to see that. The Holy Spirit finally broke through those hurts and showed me my desperate need for Jesus."

"And you accepted Him as your Savior," she stated. It wasn't a question—she knew the answer.

He nodded.

"And your brother...you know Jesus loves him. Know He was there that day to take him in His arms and bring him Home."

Logan nodded, stupid tears falling. "I know he's in Heaven and that I'll get to meet him one day." His body stiffened at the thought. Surely his brother would blame him for taking away the life that could have been his.

Em sat back, studying him. "Oh, Logan. All this time...you haven't forgiven yourself?"

He looked down, and she nudged his chin back up again. "Look at me. It was an accident. Your mom knew that. Colt obviously knew that. *I* know that, and most importantly, Jesus knows that. His heart must break for you. For what your dad put you through. For how he treated you."

"I shouldn't have climbed up there. If I could take it back..."

"You were *five*. It was an accident." Em straightened. "Wait a minute. You were afraid to tell me this—I could read it all over your face." She dipped her head to look him in the eye. "Did you think I would judge you?"

Yes. But he couldn't say that when she looked so sad at the very idea of it. "I wanted you to know," he said instead.

"I do know. I know what a good man you are."

He didn't agree, but he knew her too well to think that he'd get anywhere by arguing. He remained silent.

"You're loving and kind, and you make me want to be a better person."

"You?" He shook his head. That made no sense. "You're the best person I know."

She smiled despite the tears streaking down her face. "You're just saying that because you're mad about me."

Leave it to Em to find a way to lighten the moment. "I'm not mad about you."

Her brow furrowed.

"I love you with all my being." All his flawed being. He swallowed, waiting for Em's reply, his chest tight, squeezing the breath of anticipation from his lungs.

She blinked, her gaze one of...he couldn't tell.

"Em..." He cupped her face in his hand. "Please, say something?" *Anything.*

Tears beaded in her eyes.

Good tears or bad? Would *I love you* or *I'm sorry* follow next? His pulse whooshed through his ears.

"I..." she began. "I love you, too."

Joy rushed through him. Joy only Emmy could bring.

Leaning forward, he hovered his lips over hers, wanting to take his time, to show her how deeply and sincerely he cherished her.

Her sweet breath tickled his lips, and he couldn't wait a second longer. He pressed his lips to hers.

She kissed him back, and their kiss deepened.

Sound stopped. Even time itself seemed to pause—everything colliding into this moment.

After who-knows-how-long, she pulled back a fraction.

"What's wrong?" he asked.

"You're trembling," she murmured against his lips. "Are you okay?"

"For the first time in my life, I am."

NINETEEN

O nce they'd pulled themselves together and cleaned up the breakfast dishes, they'd driven back to San Manuel for more canvassing. Unfortunately, no one had seen the woman they were still calling Mary for lack of a better name—though Em believed "killer" suited her best. After hours of focusing on gas stations, truck stops, and a number of downright scary motels—though there had been some very well-kept ones, too—they'd made the long ride back to Rae's. They'd grabbed a bite to eat before cuddling up on the couch. Em loved Logan's strong arms around her. She could sit there, perfectly content, all night.

"Hey," he said, brushing a hair back from her face. His tender touch tickled her cheek. "Before we head to bed, there's something I'd love to show you."

"Oh?" She smiled.

"You game?"

"Always."

"That's why I love you."

"Oh, so that's the reason."

"One of many, darling," he said with a cowboy twang that sent her heart palpitating.

"So...where are we heading?"

"Nowhere in that skirt," he said.

She frowned. "What? Why?" What exactly did he have in mind? There were very few things she couldn't do in a skirt.

"You don't have a pair of jeans in that small duffel you brought from the station, do you?"

"No."

A smile tugged at the corner of his lips, and she fought not to lean over and kiss him. But she was beyond curious where they were headed and what Logan wanted to show her at 2100.

"Do you even own a pair of jeans?" he asked.

"I own pants."

He chuckled. "Not the same thing." He rubbed her knee before standing. "I've got something you can wear."

She narrowed her eyes. "I'm a little scared of what you have in mind." Both in attire and destination.

Ten minutes later, she climbed down the ladder from the loft, wearing a pair of Logan's sweats. The mishmash of blouse, sweatpants, and high-heeled boots looked... She shook her head. "I look ridiculous. Are you sure I can't ride a horse in a skirt?"

"Not unless you want to ride sidesaddle, but it's not the same experience."

"Very well, but lose that smug grin."

He pressed his fist to his mouth, but a chuckle escaped.

She dipped her chin and arched a brow.

"I'm done," he said, though he hardly looked it. He stepped closer, wrapped his arms around her, and dropped a kiss on her nose. "You're breathtaking, always."

"Better," she said, and he pressed a kiss to her lips.

He knew keeping watch despite the hour would pay off. So they were going for a nighttime horseback ride? *Perfect.* This was his opportunity. He'd prefer to kill them and hide the bodies, but Keller wanted an accident, so he'd adapted his plan, waiting for the right moment, the right situation—and this was it.

He got to his feet as they mounted their horses a hundred yards away in the pen. Climbing in his dune buggy up on the ridge, he left the lights off as he tossed his binoculars on the passenger seat. He looked at the hunting rifle strapped in place behind him and smiled. Time to do as instructed and get rid of the bothersome pair.

He watched the trail they took, then drove around the ridge to intercept them. He parked the dune buggy far enough away to stay out of their sight and earshot, then took off on foot through the woods. Soon, they'd reach the ridge. That was where the "accident" would occur—on the narrowest rim of the trail.

Em was a natural. He knew she'd be. She took to everything so easily, her easygoing nature just adapting. He loved her so. The lyrics for "I Lived" by OneRepublic tracked through his mind, especially the part about hoping the person found love and that it hurt so bad. Hurt in a good way. It was the strangest dichotomy, but he understood it. He ached for her.

"Now we're going to have to go through a narrow stretch along the trail. Just go slow."

"Where exactly are we headed?"

"There's an outcropping on the far ledge. We'll tie up the horses and head out on the boulder. Sitting there, away from any man-made lights, you can see a gazillion stars."

"A gazillion, huh?" She laughed. "Oh." Her voice went up an octave. "I see what you mean about the trail narrowing.

"You'll be good. Just let Wrangler do his thing. The horses have walked this trail so many times over the years, it's second nature to them."

Em stared down at what was visible of the steep drop-off in the moonlight. It had to be well over a hundred-foot drop.

"Easy now," Logan said. "Nice and slow. You've got this. Just trust your mount—he knows what he's doing."

A noise like the crack of a whip sounded a millisecond before the rock by Em's head shattered.

Wrangler reared back, and Logan's heart lodged in his throat. *Em.*

TWENTY

Logan hopped off Bathtub, shooing the horses forward. "Home," he said, crouching low. "Go on." The horses raced toward the ranch.

Crack. Another bullet flew overhead.

He dove low by Emmy. She lay as flat as she could make herself, her sidearm in her hand. "You okay?" he asked.

She nodded.

The flash of a muzzle shone for a second about three hundred yards due north. *Thump.* The bullet hit the dirt mere inches from the sole of his boot.

"He's too far out of range for our handguns."

"We've got to move," he said as they lay flat beneath the whoosh of another bullet overhead. "We're sitting ducks out here. Roll into the ditch." He gestured towards the ridge.

Her eyes widened. "Closer to the ledge?"

Another bullet thumped in the dirt inches from them.

Em holstered her Glock and rolled into the narrow ditch. He rolled on top of her as another bullet passed overhead, followed less than a second later by the retort.

The muzzle flash let him know the shooter was three-hundred yards away—and not a solid shot. But the shooter still had them at a great disadvantage. They were too far out of firing range and were pinned in the narrow shaft of the trail.

"We need to keep moving," he said, scooting off of Em.

Without a word, Em propped herself up on her elbows and army crawled forward.

Logan followed.

Rock shattered above them on the trail, jagged splinters raining down on them.

One hit Logan in the shoulder, but they continued moving. If they stayed still, they would die.

"Another twenty yards," he said. "and we'll line up with rocky crag and the woods."

"Got it."

Dirt clung to his face, smothering the breath from his lungs. He coughed and slithered forward, undeterred.

Fifteen yards.

Crack. Thwack.

Ten.

"Okay, stop," he hollered over the gunfire. "Right after the next shot, get upright and race for that rocky outcropping thirty feet to your ten. Keep your head low. I'll have your six."

She nodded. On the next shot, Em waited until the round hit the ground, then she crouched down and booked it for the crag.

He followed, tight and low.

Another shot and booming retort. Their attacker had moved closer, but not by much.

They braced their hands on the cold rock as they eased up, peering over it, pegging the new location of the muzzle flash.

The shooter had come in a solid twenty yards.

Em looked over, then winced at the motion.

His gut swooshed. "You're not okay."

"Just hit my head, twisted my neck when I fell off Wrangler. I'm a little dizzy, that's all. What's the plan?"

"There's a bigger crag of rocks due west, ten yards into the forest cover. We can make it there. Then...you remain, and I go hunting."

With Em as safe as possible behind the crag of boulders and tree cover, he worked his way toward the origins of the shots. Everything had been still since they hit forest cover. They'd thrown the shooter off. He was no doubt waiting for a sign of movement.

Only another twenty yards of tree coverage, and then Logan would have to work his way around rocks and onto the trail paralleling theirs.

Thump. The crack followed swiftly.

He was close.

Logan bolted from the forest cover to the first set of rocks, dropping low beneath them.

Thump. Crack. Thump. Crack.

Logan pressed his back flush with the cold rock.

The latest round hit a rock with a thwack a good dozen yards to his three o'clock.

Logan smiled. The shooter didn't know his position. And at this point, he was almost close enough to return fire.

He moved to his next position. It had minimal coverage, but he was now in range.

He waited for the shot and retort, then raised up, aimed, and fired. *One. Two. Three shots.*

Wood splintered by the shooter's position.

He crept forward, closing in.

Taking a deep breath, he held it, aimed and squeezed the trigger. *Boom.*

He waited, but the shooter didn't return fire.

He moved closer, firing again.

Again, nothing—the air eerily still.

After a steadying breath, he moved fast for his target.

He fired as he tracked forward. *Crack. Crack. Crack.*

Reaching the shooter's position. *Empty.* Untouched other than the marks in the dirt where he'd set up and his shell casings littering the ground.

An engine growled in the distance.

Logan raced towards the sound, adrenaline coursing through his legs.

He reached the edge of the forest in time to see a dune buggy disappearing in the distance.

He was too late.

TWENTY-ONE

L ogan finally got reception as they reached Aunt Rae's. Wrangler and Bathtub stood near the pen.

"Let me get you inside," Logan said to Em. "Then I'll go put them away for the night and call Tom."

She nodded, then winced.

Worry ricocheted through him.

"Stop it," she said.

"Stop what?" he asked, getting her inside and leading her to the sofa.

"Fretting. I'm fine."

"I'm calling Doc Brown all the same."

"That's overkill. It's just a bump to the head."

"It could be a concussion. Humor me."

She reached her hand to the base of her head and jerked slightly.

"Tender?" he asked, sitting beside her.

"Yeah."

"I'll get you ice."

"Look after the horses first."

"They won't go anywhere." But it was sweet that she was concerned for them.

"You take care of them, and I'll stay put," she bargained. "Deal?"

He exhaled. "Deal. But ice first." He grabbed a bag of peas from the freezer and carried them to her. "These should do the job."

"Thanks," she said, gingerly placing the bag at the base of her skull. "Now shoo."

"Keep your gun handy. I'll lock the door, just in case the shooter comes back." His gut said the shooter was long gone, but they had to remain vigilant.

"Okay," she said, refraining from nodding.

The second he was out the door, he called Tom and apprised him of the situation.

"Be there in twenty," he said.

"Thanks." Next call was to Doc Brown, who was on his way before they even hung up.

Logan strode to the pen, letting the horses in. "You guys were good today," he said, unsaddling them and letting them roll in the dirt before brushing them down.

The horses nuzzled him, and he took a brief moment to stroke each of their muzzles.

With one last goodbye to the horses, he strode back to Aunt Rae's, still very cognizant of his surroundings.

He'd barely made it inside when a car pulled up out front. He moved for the door. Gun at the ready, he opened the door a slit.

Tom had pulled the SUV along the mesa to Aunt Rae's door, bypassing the walking path from the main house. "Hey," he said, climbing out.

"Hey, man." Logan stepped back, allowing him passage.

"How's Emmy doing?" Tom asked.

"Just a little bump on the head," she said from the couch.

"Hey, Emmy," Tom said.

"Hey, Tom."

Logan shut and locked the door behind them, then joined Em on the couch.

Tom remained standing; his thumbs hooked in his belt loops. "Want to run me through it?"

Doc Brown arrived and saw to Emmy while he and Tom stepped outside to give her privacy. He took the time to bring Tom up to speed.

"I'll go collect the shells. See what other evidence I might be able to find," Tom said as Doc Brown exited Aunt Rae's.

"How is she?" he asked, his heart racing.

"I imagine she'll say she's fine." Doc Brown chuckled.

"You pegged her well," Logan said.

Tom waved and pulled out of the drive.

Logan waved and turned back to Doc.

"You should go tend to her," he said, gesturing to the barn door.

"Yes, sir."

Doc clapped him on the shoulder and headed for his car.

Taking one last breath of the crisp night air, Logan stepped inside to find Emmy still on the sofa.

"Hey, luv," he said.

She smiled. "I like when you call me that."

"Good," he said, moving to sit beside her. "Get used to it." His smile stilled. "How are you?" Doc only said that she'd claim to be okay. He hadn't actually told him how she truly was.

"I'm fine," she said as he scooted closer, concern no doubt

evident on his face. "He said he didn't see any signs of a concussion..."

"And?" Logan pressed.

"He said I'll just end up with a big goose egg and some bruising."

"And?"

She sighed. "And he told me to take it easy, keep ice on the bump, and stay awake just in case it's a concussion."

"I'm glad he's being cautious," Logan said, rubbing her knee. "I'll stay right here with you."

"Very well." She smiled. *That* smile. The mischievous one. "And how do you propose we pass the time?" she asked, scooting closer until she was right next to him.

He chuckled. "You're supposed to be taking it easy."

"I don't think he meant my lips." She leaned over, hovering hers a breath from his. She held a moment longer, then pressed them achingly slow to his.

Man, he loved this woman. He kissed her back, being extra gentle, but the more heartfelt her kiss, the deeper he fell, forgetting everything but the sweet feel of her.

Knock. Knock, Knock.

He eased back, despite wanting nothing more than to keep her wrapped up tight in his arms. "That would be Tom." He sighed, thankful for his friend but not the timing.

"Hey, Tom," Logan said, getting the door.

"Hey." Tom stepped inside.

"What'd you find?"

"Four-wheeler tracks. I followed them on foot out to the dirt road on the far side of the west pasture, but, of course, the trail ended at the pavement."

"Thanks for tracking it, though. I appreciate it."

"You're welcome, but that's not all." Tom held his Stetson in his hand and raked a hand through his hair. He looked at Em then back to Logan. "I know Emmy's recuperating, so would you rather talk outside so she can rest?"

Her head popped up from where she'd been resting it against the couch arm. "I'm good."

Tom nodded. "I found something. Hang on, I'll grab it from the SUV."

Curiosity pinged through Logan.

Tom returned with an evidence bag in hand and a pair of gloves.

Logan spied a pair of binoculars inside.

"Here you go." Tom handed him the gloves.

Logan pulled them on and then slid the binoculars out of the bag.

"I figure he lost them off the dune buggy. They were lying not far from its tracks. They look expensive," Tom said.

"They are," Logan said. "They're night vision." While the guy lacked skill shooting at long range, he certainly had at least one piece of expensive equipment. He returned them to the evidence bag.

"What are you thinking?" Tom asked. "Mary or our mystery man?"

Em kept watching over the back of the couch.

"I don't know. Whoever was shooting wasn't good, but a junkie, I'd imagine, would be far worse."

"So...you're thinking mystery man, too," Tom said.

"Seems like the more probable option." Logan lifted his chin at the evidence bag. "What I want to know is how a drifter and some guy who's hocking stuff for her has the funds for a pricey pair of binoculars like that."

Tom cocked his head. "You think someone's paying the bills?"

His gut said yes, but why and who? He shook his head. Nothing with this case was as it first appeared.

TWENTY-TWO

"**E**m," Logan murmured against her ear as they cuddled on the couch, time evaporating.

"Hmm?" Her voice was lazy and sweet like a warm summer afternoon.

"You need to get some rest." It was the last thing he wanted her to do. He wanted to hold her in his arms all night, but she needed to lay back and put ice on her head.

"Doc Brown said to stay awake," she whispered, her breath tickling his neck.

"Yes, but to take it easy, so you should probably lie down. We can watch a movie."

"Okay. After one more kiss," she said, pressing her lips to his. This kiss was different from the rest—deeper, stronger, and full of love.

He didn't want to stop, but he knew they had to. *He* had to stop. Not just because she had to rest, but because this was the woman he loved, who loved him back. Even knowing the worst of him, she still loved him back. And despite how good she felt, how good they were together, Em most certainly wasn't someone to fool around with. She never had been. She was someone to cherish. Someone to marry.

The blissful thought of marriage to Em was drowned out by an annoying *ding, ding, ding.*

"Logan," Em whispered against his lips.

"Mmm?"

"Logan." She pulled back, and cold air rushed in the warmth that had existed between them.

Ding. Ding. Ding.

What was that?

"Your phone," she said.

"Oh." He shimmied it from his pocket. "Perry," he said without bothering to look at the number.

"It's Tom."

"Hey, Tom." Logan sat straighter. "What's up?"

"Sorry to disturb you when Emmy's supposed to be resting," Tom said, "but I thought you'd want to know, we found Colt's truck."

Logan bolted upright, the burn of adrenaline surging through him. "Where?"

Em's keen gaze fixed on him.

"Hang on," he said to Tom. "I'm putting you on speaker so Em can hear, if that's all right?"

"Of course," Tom said. "Hey, ma'am...I mean, Emmy."

"Hi, Tom."

"They found Colt's truck," Logan said, catching Emmy up.

"At the bus depot in Springerville, Arizona," Tom added.

"Springerville?" Logan frowned. "After they left town, they went to San Manuel via Springerville? That would add an extra hour to the ride." He rubbed the back of his neck, trying to figure out why a woman wanting to get as far as she could from town would take a longer route to her next destination. Thinking it through some more, he added, "I wonder why it took two days to notice the truck at the bus stop. I mean, I can't picture it being a large bus station."

"Well, that's the thing," Tom said. "The service agent said the truck showed up sometime earlier today—yesterday, actually, since it's technically Monday now."

Logan frowned. "That makes no sense."

"Agreed," Tom said. "The guy works the graveyard shift. He said the truck wasn't there when he left at six a.m. but was there when he returned last night at ten."

Em cocked her head, her long hair tumbling over her shoulders. "So she dumped the truck between 0600 and 2200?"

"That's right," Tom said.

"It makes no sense." Logan scooted to the edge of the sofa. "Where has she been with the truck in the meantime? If she took it to San Manuel Saturday morning, then why on earth would she come all the way back to Springerville to dump the truck yesterday?"

"Maybe she's circling back." Em said it so simply, it took him a minute to realize what she was proposing.

"But why would she do something like that?" Tom asked.

"Running with the theory..." Em said, standing and pacing the length of the area rug. "If we hadn't learned the truck was dumped yesterday, we'd naturally assume she dumped it in Springerville Friday night after the murder, took a bus to San Manuel, had some guy hock a ring for her first thing Saturday morning, and then took the cash and made her way into a big city to either hide out or get transport somewhere else."

Logan shifted to face her. "So we'd be looking in the wrong place."

The road weaving north over Escudilla Mountain was nearly barren as they drew closer to Springerville, Arizona.

Other than the Jeep's headlights cutting a swath through the heavy fog of the shadowy mountain pass, darkness engulfed the three of them. Tom had ridden with them in Logan's Jeep so he could accompany Colt's truck back to the station garage with Max—the tow truck driver already en route.

Colt had kept Logan's old Jeep from high school in the barn for him to use whenever he was visiting Cauldron Creek. Although he always defaulted to just using Colt's truck. There was something about the old, orange Chevy pickup that he loved.

He took a steadying breath, trying to still the palpitations in his chest. *Please, Father, let the truck bring back prints.*

They needed Mary's prints to discover her true identity. Needed the man's, too. It would make them much easier to track down—so Logan could put them behind bars, where they belonged.

Thankfully, the ride passed quickly as they filled Tom in on Colt's messages and where they'd led thus far.

Logan tapped the steering wheel. If Colt was concerned enough to hide coded messages, why hadn't he said anything during one of their calls? Why hadn't he come to Logan for help?

He swallowed, guilt closing in. Why had he put his visit off until the end of February? Maybe if he'd come back sooner...if he'd been there when Mary arrived...

Em glanced over at him, concern on her brow visible in the light from an oncoming car.

He didn't have to say a word. Just shrugged a shoulder, and she knew that meant they'd talk later. It was not a conversation he'd want to have with anyone but Em, despite what a good friend Tom was.

Pulling into the bus station, he caught sight of Colt's truck, and a weight crushed his chest, ripping the breath from his lungs.

Em reached over, resting a hand on his leg.

He swallowed, his throat tighter than before. This was going to be gut-punch painful.

Three buses sat out front. One parked and empty. Two preparing to leave.

"I guess they still run around the clock," Emmy said.

Logan shifted the Jeep into Park and cut the ignition, his gaze landing once again on Colt's truck. A wave of emotions sloshed through his gut. His last time riding in the truck had been with Colt during his fall visit—driving into town to buy freshly roasted Hatch green-and-red chile ristras to hang from the porch. Fall in New Mexico was his favorite time of year—the New Mexico State Fair, Albuquerque International Balloon Fiesta, the delicious smell of fresh chiles roasting, the bite in the night air, the yellow Aspens. It'd been a great visit—though he'd had no idea it would be his last with Colt. Would he have done anything different if he'd known? Said more? Done more? He shook his head. He couldn't go there; he'd lived with regret long enough. It was time he embraced the freedom he had in Christ. Colt would have wanted him to. And their last visit really had been a good one. That...*those* good memories are what mattered.

"Let's grab some gloves and take a look while we wait for Max," Tom said. "If we see anything, great, but the full processing will take place in the station garage."

Em and Logan nodded.

Gloves on, they opened the truck...and the scent of sunflower seeds and root beer wafted out.

Logan's breath caught. *Colt.*

"I'm sorry, man." Tom clapped him on the shoulder.

"I know. Thanks." Colt had been a huge part of Tom's life, too.

Concern hung thick on Em's brow, but she didn't say a word—just communicated her love and compassion through the depths of her soulful eyes.

"You ready?" Tom asked, snapping the wrist of the gloves tightly in place.

Logan nodded.

"You take the driver's side," Tom instructed Logan. "Emmy, you take the passenger side, and I'll take the covered truck bed."

The three moved to their assigned locations and began searching. Fingerprinting would happen back at the station garage. This was simply to see if anything of interest had been left behind.

His flashlight on, Logan bent, looking under the seat, running a hand along the floorboard as Em did the same on her side, their heads nearly bumping a time or two.

"I've got something!" Em's voice rose in pitch.

Logan straightened, and Tom rounded the truck bed.

"What is it?" Tom asked.

"A wadded-up gum wrapper. Here," she said, moving back so Tom could see it. She angled her flashlight right on the silver wrapper wedged between the seat and the floorboard.

"Colt hated gum," Logan said, his voice a little strangled.

Tom left it in place and took a picture on his cell phone of the wrapper, which appeared to have a used wad of gum tucked inside. Then he took pictures of the surrounding area. "This is going to shift when the truck is towed. I'm going to grab an evidence bag from the SUV. I'll be right back."

Logan smiled. "You know what this means?" he asked Em.

She smiled back. "DNA."

TWENTY-THREE

"This place is gross," Mary said, eyeing the faded, sixties-style tie-dyed quilt on the motel room bed, which dipped visibly in the middle.

"It's out of the way," Jeff said. He started to drop the duffel they shared on the floor, apparently thought better of it, and dropped it on the round, faux-wood table. "You're supposed to be in Mexico, remember?"

"Dude, do you know how many women go missing from there every year? I'm not taking my chances. Besides, we already agreed I'm not going." She narrowed her eyes. "Why did we have to change motels again? What's wrong?"

"Nothing. Just...if *he* finds out you're still here, we're both dead."

"He's not going to find out. As far as he knows, I'm already there."

"You better hope nothing happens to clue him in, or it's both our necks."

"You're worrying over nothing. If he hasn't figured it out

yet, then he's not going to." She grabbed her toiletries kit from the duffel and headed for the bathroom. "Besides, he doesn't scare me like he does you."

"Because you haven't seen what he's capable of," he said, following her into the puke-pink bathroom.

She fished out her toothbrush and paste and set to work brushing her teeth, leaving the water running to hopefully heat up. But hot water in a dive like this was a luxury that probably didn't exist. She was tired of living like a transient. It'd been too many years. He'd promised the money would roll in, but so far there had been very little—just enough to eke out an existence, despite the fact that they were taking all the risks.

Jeff stepped back into the main room, pacing and muttering to himself.

She couldn't hear him over the water, which was just as well. He worried too much. Splashing the lukewarm water on her face, she scrubbed with soap, happy to see her own face again. The hoodie could be burned for all she cared. Over a month in it, and she was done.

Shutting off the water, Jeff's muttering reached her ears.

She strode back into the bedroom area. "Dude. Stop stressing. He isn't going to find out I'm here. If you're that worried about it, then let's run. We could head north, hit the Canadian border."

"He said I need to stay here. Need to make sure everything goes the way we planned it."

"Why? Who's going to figure out the real reason behind it? I mean, come on. So one old man got wise. You know how many we've duped. It was *one* guy."

"Yeah, and that one guy has a special agent as a grandson."

"What?" She stilled. "He's with the feds?"

"No. The boss said the grandson and his lady friend are with the Coast Guard."

"What?" She laughed, sitting on the bed. It squeaked beneath her petite form.

"Yeah. Yuk it up. He's a special investigator with the Coast Guard."

"So he investigates fishing violations." She scoffed. "What's the big deal?"

"You really are stupid."

She stood, strode to him, and slapped his cheek.

He grabbed her, holding the fleshy part of her upper arm in a vise. "Don't. Ever. Do. That. Again."

She tugged her arm away. "Then stop calling me stupid."

"Stop *acting* stupid. I don't know what all Coast Guard agents handle, but these two know what they're doing, and Keller is getting mad."

"It's not our fault if they're good."

"No. but..."

"But what?" she pressed.

"But he's already fuming. He finds out you're still around, and I don't want to see how angry he'll get."

"*Oooh.* He'll be angry," she mocked.

"Trust me. You don't want to cross him. I know what happened to the last guy who did."

She frowned. "What are you talking about?"

"The guy he had handling the claims and working the scam before me," Jeff said.

"Yeah? What about him?" she asked.

He looked at her, fear evident in his brown eyes. "He's dead."

Mary shifted her weight forward, the bed squeaking again.

"What do you mean? As in, Keller killed him?"

Jeff raked a shaky hand through his spiky hair. "Don't say his name."

"Why? It's not even his real one."

Jeff's jaw stiffened. "How do you know that?"

"Let's just say I like to have an ace up my sleeve."

"You better be careful."

"Or what?"

"You could end up like the last guy. We both could."

"Logan," Em said as they headed back for Cauldron Creek and the ranch—the roads dark, the hour late. Unfortunately, no one at the bus station recognized Mary, which only perpetuated Emmy's belief that Mary had changed her appearance in some way.

"Yes?" he said, looking over.

"I was just thinking...maybe it was good Tom called when he did. In addition to finding the truck, I mean." She bit her bottom lip, heat flushing her cheeks. This was an awkward conversation to have, but if she couldn't be open and honest with Logan, then how could they move forward? And she most definitely wanted to move forward with him.

"What do you mean?" he said as the solemn dark of night engulfed them.

"I'm just not sure how far we would have gone without Tom's call interrupting us." She bit her bottom lip. She wasn't pointing fingers; she'd been equally culpable for getting too wrapped up in kissing. She loved Logan, wanted to be close to him, but her faith and her self-respect both demanded that she put limits on how far she let things go for now.

"We both know there's a line we won't cross because of our love of God and our commitment to choosing His best for us. His best is marriage. We have our whole lives before us. I trust nothing more than kissing would have happened. Don't you?"

She didn't answer right away, and his expression shifted from confidence to concern. "Em? Are you all right?"

"I'm sorry. I'm still stuck on the marriage part." He'd said marriage, right?

He gripped her hand tighter. "Does the thought of marriage to me scare you?"

"No." The complete opposite, but... "I just had no idea that you were thinking along those lines."

He shifted to face her. "You didn't think I was just fooling around, did you?" Pain shone in his eyes. "I'm not that guy anymore—and I'd never be that way with you."

"With me?"

"I love you, Em. I never would have told you how I feel if I wasn't prepared to offer you the kind of commitment you deserve. You're priceless to me."

Priceless? Warmth spread through her chest.

"Of course I want to marry you," he said. "That is, if you'll have me."

"Have you?" Tears glistened in her eyes, and she noticed that he held his breath. Marrying Logan would be a dream come true. A long-held dream—one she'd tucked away in her heart for years. But now Logan had become the man she'd always known he was inside, and he loved her. "Of course I'd marry you." She bit her bottom lip. Had she just agreed to marry Logan?

He brought their intertwined hands to his mouth and pressed a kiss to her fingers. "Good. Hold onto that answer."

She frowned.

He chuckled. "You can't expect me to settle for such a poor proposal."

"I wouldn't call it poor."

He released a laugh. "Look around us, Em. We're driving in

the dark, in the middle of nowhere, tracking a murderess. Trust me, I will do far better."

This time, she brought their hands to her lips and pressed a kiss to his cold fingers. "And I'll hold you to it."

TWENTY-FOUR

After a solid nap followed by a hearty breakfast, Em stood and moved to the coffee table. She lifted the paper with the phone numbers on it. Though she had typed them in her phone, it never hurt to double-check.

"I'll call the Medicare office to see if anyone there recalls talking with your grandpa. It's a long shot, but they might be willing to share what the calls pertained to."

"I'll call the medical supply store and ask the same thing."

"Great," she said, looking back at Colt's code. "You know what's still bugging me?"

"What's that?" he asked, lifting his phone off the charger on the end table.

"The dates after the numbers make no sense."

He narrowed his eyes, scooting closer to examine the notes with her.

"Look," she said. "4/23, 5/21, and 6/31."

"Six-thirty-one?" Logan frowned. "There are only thirty days in June."

"And the other dates are so far back that it seems odd

timing. If Colt was looking into something, wouldn't you expect the calls to have happened closer together? Hang on..." She pulled her calendar up on her phone. "Okay, that's even weirder."

"What?"

"The April and May dates both fall on a Saturday if we're looking at this past year. I could see calling a hospital on a weekend, but Medicare offices are closed."

"So what are you thinking?"

"What if they aren't really dates?" she said. "What if they're extension numbers split up to look like dates?"

"That's brilliant, Em," he said. "Give it a try with the Medicare number."

"Will do." She dialed, then input the extension...and the line rang.

"Ms. Overman," a lady answered on the second ring.

Em gave Logan a thumbs-up, and he nodded. They were getting closer to the truth. She could feel it.

"Hello, I'm Special Agent Emmalyne Thorton, working in cooperation with the Cauldron County Sheriff's Department. I'm calling in regard to a phone call we believe was made to you by Mr. Colt Tucker."

"Colt Tucker..." *Tap. Tap. Tap.* Nails drumming on a desk, perhaps? "Of course, I know Mr. Tucker."

"You do?" She smiled and glanced over at Logan with a wink.

"Yes. Sweet man. How is he doing?" Ms. Overman asked.

"I'm afraid..." How on earth did she put this delicately? Devoid of any ideas, she simply stated the fact. "I'm sorry to have to tell you this, but I'm afraid he's been murdered."

"Murdered? Oh my word. That's terrible."

"Could you tell my colleague and me what he called about? We're investigating his case," Em said.

She switched the call to speaker, so Logan could hear, too, as he hadn't dialed the medical supply company yet. He placed his phone back on the charging base and scooted closer to Em, his shoulder rubbing hers.

"I remember the calls well," Ms. Overman said. "He was quite upset that his wife's information had been used in recent Medicare claims. One for a wheelchair vehicle lift, one for a prosthetic limb, and one for a scooter."

"Ma'am, this is Special Agent Logan Perry here," he said, introducing himself. "I'm Colt's grandson."

"Oh. How terrible to work your grandfather's case." Ms. Overman's voice spiked an octave.

Em rubbed Logan's arm. The toll it was taking on him was evident, but she'd work the case, too, if it had been a loved one of hers—no matter how difficult the experience would prove.

"It's not easy," Logan said. "But it's necessary." He cleared his throat. "As far as the Medicare claims, my grandma used all three items by the end of her life, but she's been deceased for years."

"Correct, and these claims were filed a few months ago. Mr. Tucker feared there were more out there that he hadn't discovered yet."

"Is it possible someone made a mistake?" Em asked, just to cover the bases.

"It's possible..." Ms. Overman said. "But so is the strong possibility someone is committing fraud. Mr. Tucker feared the latter and called me. I flagged it for our fraud department, but I'll warn you, they are extremely backlogged. Unfortunately, Medicare fraud is a very lucrative business."

"How lucrative?" Logan asked.

"Well, if we look at the items your grandpa called about, the Universal Power Wheelchair Lift by Harmar retails for over two thousand dollars. The scooter was from a top-of-the-line brand, so we're looking at another four thousand—but the prosthetic limb is where the real money is. The model on the claim runs for sixty-thousand dollars."

"My grandfather jotted down some numbers along with your contact information. I'm wondering if they could be the claim numbers for those items," he said.

Em understood the need for his question. He wanted to be sure he understood all of Colt's codes. His grandfather had hidden those messages for him in case the worst happened—and it had. Now it was up to them to see that justice was done.

TWENTY-FIVE

"Could I read them out?" Em asked Ms. Overman. "Or could you let us know the claim numbers?"

"Absolutely," she said. "I'm thrilled to learn two special agents are on the case. As I said, it could be a long time before the fraud department can investigate Mr. Tucker's claims. Here we go..." She read off the rows of numbers.

Em and Logan followed along on the number puzzle clutched in her hand. Ms. Overman's numbers matched the ones on Colt's paper exactly.

"Does that help?" Ms. Overman asked.

"More than you know," Em said.

"Is there a doctor of record on the claims?" Logan asked.

Logan prayed that the answer would be yes.

"Yes. A doctor Kenneth Sighn from the pain management team within the Orthopedics Department at Albuquerque General."

"Is that unusual?" Em asked. "I mean for a prosthetic limb, in particular, to come from the Ortho Department?"

"Typically, the claim for a limb comes straight from the

prosthetics department, but the pain management division of the ortho department works closely with amputees, so it's not unheard of. And the wheelchair ramp can come straight from the pain management team." A chime sounded in the background. "Oh, I'm sorry. That was my reminder." The chirping stopped. "I've got an important team meeting, so I best scoot."

"Thank you for all your help," Em said.

"I'm glad I could help. And thank you for seeing this through. I know it would have meant a lot to him," Ms. Overman said. "I still can't believe he's gone. We just spoke three days ago."

The day of Colt's murder? "I'm guessing that was a follow-up call?" Em asked, her brows pinched.

"Yes. The first call came in a number of weeks back, then Mr. Tucker called back three days ago to see if the case had gotten any traction. I'm so sorry, but I really must go."

"You've been extremely helpful. Truly, thank you so much," she said before Ms. Overman disconnected the call.

Em looked over at Logan. "Give Tucson Medical Supply a call, and let's hope they're just as helpful."

Logan dialed Tucson Medical Supply Company. It was the shop where Mee-Maw had gotten all her necessary medical equipment, though it had been years since they'd been in the store. He doubted anyone working there would remember Mee-Maw or their family. He put the call on speaker so Em could hear, too.

"Tucson Medical Supply," a man answered.

"Hi. This is Special Agent Logan Perry—"

"Logan, hi. This is Paul Gaines. I don't know if you remember me. It's been a number of years."

"Of course I remember you."

"I just heard about Colt." Paul sighed. "My deepest condolences, Logan."

"Thank you. I appreciate it." He truly did, but he had to stay on point. It was how he could best serve Colt. He was about to shift into asking questions, but Paul spoke before he could.

"It's so hard to believe he's gone when I just spoke with him."

"You did? Could you share what you two talked about?"

"Of course. I got a Medicare claim for a prosthetic leg for your grandmother, a wheelchair lift for her vehicle, and a scooter. I knew it had to be a mistake, but I called Colt to let him know it'd come across my desk."

"How long ago was this?" Logan asked.

"Oh, about three weeks back."

Not long before he'd spoken with Colt for the last time. He still didn't understand why he hadn't said anything.

"I assumed it was a mistake," Paul continued. "Things like that can happen. But Colt called me back three days ago."

Logan's body went rigid. The day of the murder? "What time?"

"Oh, around lunchtime."

"And what did he say?" Logan squeezed Emmy's hand.

"Hang on just a minute," Paul said.

"Sure. No problem." Logan looked at Em and shrugged.

Swishing sounded, voices muted in the background, and then a door shut. "I apologize," Paul said, "but there are lots of customers on the floor. Better to continue our conversation from my office."

"Of course," Logan said.

"He said he called Medicare," Paul began, "and that they were investigating for potential fraud. Colt asked if there was anything I could do in the meantime, as Medicare was really backlogged, so I offered to call the ordering physician myself.

Not sure why that was so hard for Medicare to do, but you know...all that red tape."

"And who was the ordering physician?" Logan asked, curious if the name matched up with what Ms. Overman had said.

"A Doctor Sighn in the Ortho Department at Albuquerque General. When I called, they put me on with the office manager. She said it was clearly a mistake. Probably an entry clerk new at the job, entering ID numbers wrong. Your grandmother's social security number wasn't the only error. The ordering physician on the claim, Dr. Sighn, died several years ago."

Shock roiled through Logan. What on earth? The fraud Colt became aware of clearly went deep. "Do you remember who you spoke to?" he asked.

"I'm afraid not. I speak with so many hospitals and doctors' offices. But I did let Colt know the office manager said it'd just been a mistake—not that he seemed willing to accept that."

"What gave you that impression?" Logan asked.

"He told me straight out that he was certain it was fraud."

"And what do you think?"

Paul sighed. "I don't know what to think."

TWENTY-SIX

L ogan took a hot shower while Emmy called the Ortho Department at Albuquerque General. Returning to the living room, he found her off the phone, bent over the coffee table and scribbling in her notepad.

"I'm going to make some tea. Would you like a cup?" he asked.

She looked up at him and smiled, but it was that distracted smile that said she was deep in thought. "Yes, please."

He set to work making the tea. When it was ready, he carried over the mugs and set Em's on the coffee table. "How did your calls go?"

"I was able to speak briefly with all three doctors on the pain management team."

"And?"

"Dr. Geoul was arrogant. O'Rourke was nice. And Keller kept saying he was too busy to talk, but he at least answered my basic questions."

"Any feelings based on your conversations?" Em always

had gut feelings—and nine times out of ten, her intuition was right.

"Something about Dr. Keller didn't sit right with me, but I can't pinpoint why."

"We need to run background checks, do some digging on all three. I'll do it. Why don't you lay down, get some more rest than the short nap we took," Logan said, knowing even as he made the suggestion that it wasn't going to fly.

"I'll sleep later. This is too important." She was so frustratingly stubborn, but he loved her steadfastness. Loved her, stubbornness and all. As soon as all of this was over and the people responsible for Colt's murder were in jail, he was going to properly propose and marry her. He'd been dreaming of it for years. Only now, he was finally the man she deserved for him to be.

She narrowed her beautiful eyes. "What are you thinking about?" she asked, setting her tea mug on a coffee table coaster.

"Not what. *Who*," he said, doing the same with his mug, the steam still curling up in wisps.

"I don't understand," she said.

"It's not *what* I'm thinking about." He scooted closer to her. "It's *who* I'm thinking about." He cupped her face, caressing her cheek. "I know this isn't the right time, but I can't help myself."

She leaned into him, and he brought his lips to hers. Just for one kiss, just for a second.

A blur of minutes later, she eased back, breaking the mind-boggling kiss.

"As amazing as that was..." She swallowed, slipping a loose strand of hair behind her ear. "We'd better get back to the case."

"Right," he said, shaking himself out of his stupor. "Let's run the docs, and then we both rest, deal?"

"Deal," she said. "If I can sleep, that is. I'm so disgusted to think of how many fake claims whoever is behind this has probably filed. How much money they've stolen. How many people they've harmed...or possibly killed."

"I know that's what happened to Colt." He knew it with all his being. "This is so much more than a robbery gone wrong. He uncovered the fraud, and the person behind it either killed him or had someone do it for him."

"Mary or our mystery man?" she said.

"I'm not sure which pulled the trigger, but I'm leaning more towards our mystery man, given he had no qualms in trying to kill us."

"Agreed," she said.

An hour of research and digging later, Logan looked over at Em. "None of them have a criminal record, but something strange popped up about Dr. Keller."

She arched her delicate brows. "Oh?"

"I can't find anything concrete on Dr. Mark Keller beyond two years ago. No driver's license outside of when he got one in New Mexico, no past home address, even the med school listed on his medical license doesn't have any record of a Mark Keller attending. It's like he came out of nowhere. However, there was a Dr. Markus Keller that came up during my search. It's definitely not the same guy—Markus Keller died six years ago—but he *did* attend the same medical college at the same time that our Dr. Mark Keller says he did."

"You think he took on Markus Keller's identity of sorts? If so, maybe he knew him in the past?"

"It's certainly possible. But without a real name to go on, it'll be hard to say when or where they could have connected."

"Hmm," Em said, and he could see the wheels spinning. Her mind was fascinating and alluring as all get out. "My gut says there's definitely more there."

"I'll dig deeper on Dr. Markus Keller."

"Good plan," she said, leaning forward. She lifted Colt's

last number puzzle from the stack of notes. "And, we still have the last number puzzle to solve."

"True." He scooted close enough to read it with her. He'd take a look, then dive back into researching. He studied it and blinked. "Could it really be that simple?"

"You solved it already?"

"Yeah. I can't believe I didn't catch it right away. Colt used to leave these latitude and longitude puzzles around—they'd lead me on a scavenger hunt to find something he'd hidden. He mixed these up in a different formation than what I'm used to, but still, I should have seen it."

"So, it's like 'X marks the spot'?" she asked.

"Yes." He pulled out his phone, opened an app, and typed in the coordinates. "Aspen Lake."

She rubbed his back. "Is that far from here?"

"No. Only about a half hour."

"Maybe we should visit?" she said. "See if we can find any link between the town and Colt?"

"Or a tie between Colt and what got him killed."

TWENTY-SEVEN

"Stay put," Jeff said, as he parked outside of the convenience store. It was nearly midnight. The place should be empty enough that no one would notice Mary waiting in the car. And at this hour, the owner would be bored and tired. As long as Jeff was in and out fast and kept his face hidden, the guy wouldn't pay any attention to him.

He looked over at Mary. "I'll be back in a minute," he said. "Keep your head down." It was late and dark, but they still couldn't risk her being seen. Her picture was plastered all over the news. Why he was helping her—and risking ticking off the boss—he didn't fully understand. He wasn't a nice guy, but there was something about the girl that stayed his hand.

"Get me Doritos," she hollered from the car.

He waved his arm to indicate he heard her and pulled his hood up as he entered the convenience store.

The owner eyed him warily.

He moved through the store as quickly as possible, just getting a few things to munch on for the night.

Turning to walk down the last aisle, he froze in his tracks.

What was she doing in here? He strode forward, grabbing her by the arm. "I told you to stay in the car."

"Ow. You're hurting me." She squirmed in his hold.

The shop owner leaned to the side, his gaze fixed on them.

"Get back in the car. *Now*," he whispered hard against her ear.

"I want some Tylenol PM or NyQuil. I need something to sleep. It's been days."

"Fine." His fingers bit into the flesh on her arms. "I'll grab some. Now get back in the car."

As she stomped toward the door, her hoodie slipped off. She quickly swiped it up again, but the damage had been done. The owner had seen her.

She rushed out.

Jeff turned on the owner, reaching for his gun.

Terror radiated in the clerk's eyes. "You don't have—"

Two shots and he dropped the guy.

A moment later, Jeff climbed in the car and turned the ignition.

"Are you crazy?" she asked as he reversed out of the spot. "You didn't have to kill him."

"He recognized you from the news. I could see it in his eyes. I didn't have a choice," he said, peeling out of the parking lot, loose asphalt pinging the car. "His death is on your hands. Not mine."

"I didn't pull the trigger," she said. "This is getting out of control."

"I just saved your life, so be grateful, you hear me?"

She pulled her knees to her chest, not saying a word.

"If he reported you, it would have ruined both of us. Even if the cops didn't nab us, Keller would know you didn't follow the plan, and then we'd both be dead." He sped down the highway, bypassing the exit for their motel.

"Hey, my things are there," she said.

"There's no time to stop. I don't want us within fifty miles of that gas station by the time the cops get there. We need to find another place to hole up."

Something chirped.

Logan rolled over. Was it morning already? Were those birds singing?

Chirp. Chirp. Chirp.

Ugh. His nighttime ringtone. It was less jarring than the daytime *ding*, but no ringtone was pleasant when awoken in the night.

He reached over to the nightstand, fumbling to grab his cell.

"Yeah?" he answered.

"It's Tom."

Logan sat up in bed and rubbed the sleep from his eyes. "What's up?"

"They spotted her."

Thank You, Lord.

He kicked his legs over the side of the bed, adrenaline already sizzling through his limbs. "Where?"

"At Bobby's convenience store in Bosque," Tom said, then paused. "The guy with her shot Bobby." Anger vibrated in his voice. "Paramedics are en route."

Logan pinched the bridge of his nose. "Not Bobby." They'd all played ball growing up in the small town. "Is he going to be okay?"

"I don't know. He managed to call the station and then must have blacked out. I'll know more when paramedics arrive," Tom said. "I'm already on my way and I'm calling in surrounding law enforcement to help us with the hunt. We've got a window here. I don't want to blow it."

Logan raked a hand through his hair. "We'll be on our way asap."

Knock. Knock.

"Hey, Em," he said, clicking on the nightstand lamp.

"Okay to come in?" she called out.

"Yep." He stood, moving for his shirt on the back of the desk chair.

She opened the bedroom door, the hall light spilling in, mixing with the soft glow of the bedside lamp. She opened her mouth to speak, but when her gaze fixed on him, she just stood there, silent.

After a moment, she cleared her throat, her cheeks flushing pink. "I was getting a glass of water when I heard your cell. Is everything okay?"

"That was Tom," he said, grabbing his knit t-shirt and sliding it on. "They spotted her."

Em's eyes widened. "Where?"

"About an hour from here."

"I'll get dressed," she said.

"I will too." PJ bottoms weren't going to cut it.

Em turned and headed into the hall, closing his door behind her.

He swapped out his PJs for a pair of jeans and pulled a long-sleeve Henley over his t-shirt. Grabbing his gun, he holstered it and snatched his keys off the desk.

This was it.

Please, Lord, don't let her slip through our fingers.

"Why is she still here?" Keller roared.

"She said she was scared to go over the border alone," Jeff said, pacing by the vending machine at the end of the motel corridor, wondering how far Keller was going to take this. Kill the girl for sure. Attempt to kill him? That was the burning question on his mind.

"You know what you have to do," Keller said.

Jeff hesitated. He liked the girl. No clue why, but he did. But she'd boxed him in. He had no choice. "I understand," he finally said, his tone non-committal to his own ears.

"I want to hear it. Just so we're clear. Repeat after me. I will kill her and make sure her body is not found."

Jeff scoped out his surroundings again. All the room windows visible from the vending machine were pitch black. The parking lot was devoid of life.

"Say it!" Keller yelled.

One last glance at his surroundings. "I will kill her and make sure her body is never found." It was too late for being Mr. Nice Guy. She'd brought this on herself. It was either her or both of them, and as much as he liked the girl, she certainly wasn't worth dying for.

"Good," Keller clipped. "Now get it done!"

The call dropped.

Balling his hands into fists, Jeff strode to the stolen sedan, the plates flipped. If he was going to do this, he needed some liquid courage first. Whiskey would do.

He climbed in the car and slammed the door. He'd follow Keller's orders. But he wasn't going to enjoy squeezing the life from the girl. Turning the ignition, he reversed out of the parking slot and flew down the road. He was getting tired of Keller's demands.

TWENTY-EIGHT

Filled to the brim with Jack Daniel's, Jeff swaggered toward the motel room door, cursing quietly to himself when he noticed the light slipping through a crease in the window curtains. She was still awake. Not what he'd been hoping to find. It would have been so much easier with her asleep so he wouldn't have to look into her eyes. He shook out his hands, fingers that would soon be biting into her throat.

Strangle her or crush her windpipe? One was faster—less frightening, he'd imagine. He didn't have any choice about taking her out, but he didn't have to be cruel about it.

He turned the knob and found it locked, as instructed. He'd knock, but it would do no good. He'd instructed her not to open it for anyone. He rummaged through his jean pockets, trying to recall which pocket he'd put the room key in. Finally, his hand wrapped around it. It took him a fumbling moment to get the key in the door and turn the knob. He staggered into the room, shutting and locking the door behind him. No Mary. He looked to the bathroom—the door was closed, the light on.

He stepped to the door, able to hear the shower running.

He weighed his options but decided against killing her in the shower. She'd be slippery beneath his hands. He'd wait until she came out, and then he'd do the deed.

Sitting on the edge of the bed that creaked beneath his weight, he took another swig, growing impatient. What was taking her so long?

His muscles coiled as a few more minutes slipped by.

She never took long showers. Always quick. Always uncomfortable being vulnerable.

"Hey, Mary," he hollered.

No answer.

Enough of this. Setting the bottle on the nightstand, he stood and strode to the bathroom. Looked like he'd be killing her in the shower after all.

He turned the knob. Locked. "Mary!"

No answer.

He jiggled the handle. "Let me in."

Nothing but the sound of the shower running.

He rammed the door with his shoulder. Once. Twice. The third time did the trick, busting the lock. He stumbled in the room full of steam. He pulled back the curtain...and his stomach flipped. She was gone. Heat seared his limbs.

Turning around, he found a note taped to the mirror.

I heard you. I'm not going to be another one of Keller's kills.

Cussing, he bolted from the room.

When he found her... He no longer cared about making her death merciful—or quick.

L ogan's cell rang, and he answered on Bluetooth. "Hey, Tom."

"A motel manager just called. Said he spotted the woman.

She left his establishment on foot not long ago. It's the Grand Sunshine Motel in Duro. I'm still up in Bosque, and Denton is about forty minutes out. Please tell me you're close."

"We're about twenty from there," Logan said, swinging a U-turn, his tires squealing. "But I can make up some time." He depressed the accelerator.

Fifteen minutes and a racing heart later, Logan held the glass door of the Grand Sunshine Motel open for Em.

"Thanks." She stepped inside, taking in her surroundings. Blue shag carpet was squishy under her heels, the walls were covered with faded floral wallpaper, and the reception desk was made of brown paneling with a darker brown countertop.

A man dressed in a brown-and-tan bowling shirt with the name Lyle stitched in orange on it looked up from the counter.

"You folks want a room? We rent by the hour or the night." He looked up at them and smiled, his coffee-stained teeth crooked on the bottom. "I'm guessing you're in for the night." He chuckled.

Em's skin crawled. *Ewww.*

"We're not looking for a room," Logan explained. "We're looking for her." Logan slid the picture of the woman over. "You called the sheriff?"

"Yeah, but you ain't Tom."

"No, I'm not." He gestured between himself and Em. "We're special agents assisting on the case." He held up his badge, and she did the same. "You're welcome to call Tom to verify," he suggested at the man's hesitance.

"Nah, I'm good. And yeah, I seen her. She came around the corner, looking back the other way. Nearly bowled me over. So skittish."

"She say anything to you?" Em asked.

"Yeah. Said the guy she came in with was a mean drunk,

the abusive sort. She begged me not to tell him which way she went or that I'd seen her."

"And?"

"I didn't. But she was right. He sure was mean. Came flying out of that room, hollering for her."

"He say her name?" Em asked, hopeful.

"I ain't gonna say what he called her." He looked Em over. "Not in front of a lady," he added.

"Did he come in here?" Logan asked.

"Yeah. He reeked of whiskey. Asked if I'd seen where the girl went."

"And?"

"I played dumb."

"And he bought it?" Logan asked.

"Seemed to. Got in his car and sped out of here. Though he went left, and she'd gone right."

"Time is of the essence," Logan said. "I'm going to need the make and model of his car."

"A black Toyota Corolla. Maybe a decade old. The bumper hung low on the right. Plate number HQN-175."

Logan blinked, clearly taken aback. "That's extremely detailed information, Lyle."

"I have an eye for detail." He leaned forward, looked both ways, then said low beneath his breath, "I deal with a lot of unsavory characters here. I pay close attention. Even got secret cameras hidden throughout the parking lot and outside corridors. Not to mention Bessie behind the counter."

Logan hiked a brow. "Bessie?"

Lyle lifted a .38 special revolver on top of the counter.

"Okay, then," Logan said. "Last two questions. What's out here in the direction the woman went? Where might she have gone?"

"She'd probably be looking for a bus station, truck stop..." Em said.

"The Stop N Sup is about a quarter a mile to the right," Lyle said. "She's a smart one." He looked at Logan and winked. "I'd keep her."

Keep her? Em took a deep inhale, keeping her temper in check. The man was crass, but he was also being helpful.

"If she turned around and started heading to the left, she'd get to the Brown Hen motel and, beyond that, the '77 Truck Stop."

"Thanks, Lyle." Logan tapped the counter, then held the door for Em on the way out.

"Is there any kind of reward?" Lyle asked.

"Helping catch a criminal is a reward in and of itself," Logan said as the door swung shut behind them.

TWENTY-NINE

L ogan pulled into the Stop N Sup truck stop.
Emmy glanced around at the rows of tractor cabs settled in for the night, most with their parking lights on.

"Where do we start?" she asked.

"I'll take the right. You take the left and start knocking."

She nodded and did as Logan had said, knocking on the door of one semi after another, apologizing for waking the driver, then asking each trucker if they'd seen the woman in the printout Emmy had brought along. About five tractor cabs in, the driver held up a finger midway through Em's explanation. "Let me help you out, darlin'." He lifted the radio, tweaked the frequency, and cleared his throat. "It's Hank. I've got a special agent here at the Stop N Sup looking for a woman who's wanted for murder. She's blonde, white, petite, and she would have hitched a ride..." He looked back at Em.

"Probably ten, maybe fifteen minutes ago," she said.

"I saw her," a woman's voice said. "Selling herself for a ride."

"Now, Rita," a man said on the other end. "She wasn't selling herself. She just needed a ride."

"Uh-huh. Sure."

The driver set the radio back in its holder on the dash. "That's the O'Briens. Three cabs to the left," he said, pointing toward the crystal-blue tractor.

"Thanks so much," Em said. She flagged Logan down, and they approached the O'Briens' tractor together.

Logan was lifting his hand to knock when the driver's side door swung open. A woman emerged, in pink curlers with a clear shower cap over them and a pink, fluffy robe. She started speaking before they could say a word. "I knew that thing was trouble the moment I laid eyes on her."

A balding man with an orange beard appeared behind her. "Herman O'Brien," he said, extending his hand. "You've met my wife, Rita."

"Special Agents Perry and Thorton," Logan said, shaking the man's hand. Em followed.

"Special agents." The woman clutched her chest. "Are we in some sort of danger?"

"I'd keep your cab locked up tight tonight, just in case." No doubt, that man would come looking for the woman. Em prayed he'd leave the truckers alone, that he wouldn't harm anyone else.

Herman retrieved a shotgun from the cab. "This is just one of several," he said, holding it up. "No one will bother us tonight."

Logan nodded.

"Hank said something about murder?" Rita said.

"Yes. The woman is wanted in connection to a murder," Em said.

Rita gasped. Actually gasped. "I knew something was wrong about her from the moment I saw those big eyes poking out from under her hoodie. She tried to keep her face hidden, but I said she had to look at me if she wanted my help. She did, and I saw her eyes. Soulless eyes, I'm telling you. Sent a chill right up my spine. I won't be forgetting those in a hurry."

Em held up the printout. "This was her?"

"Yes, ma'am...agent...special agent," the woman scrambled.

"Emmy, please," she said.

"Rita." She nodded. "But you already knew that."

"Do you know where she went?" Logan asked.

"Yes..." Her face pinched. "Oh, poor Matt. I told that young fellow not to give rides to hitchers, but he never listens."

"Matt?" Em asked.

"Matt Hartson," Herman said, finally getting a word in edgewise. "He's new to the gang. Only been driving a rig for a couple years."

Em supposed in relation to the age of some of the other truckers, a couple years in the field seemed young.

"Can you describe his rig for us? Which way he went? How long ago?" The questions tumbled out of Logan's mouth rapid-fire.

"We sure can," Herman said. "He's got a purple, sparkly cabin—stands out like a sore thumb. And he's pulling a tractor for XPC."

"Like the printer company?" Em clarified.

"Yes, ma—Emmy," Rita said. "Got a big, gold-and-white XPC symbol on either side."

"And they went which direction?" she asked.

"Heading on 180 toward Silver City about ten minutes ago."

Had Matt heard Hank's call for the woman? Had she? And, if so, what would she do? Was she armed? Em sent up a prayer for Matt. "The radio frequency Hank used, is that for—"

"It's just for those camped out here for the night," Herman said.

Em's taut shoulders loosened.

"We use a different one on the road," he elaborated.

So they still had the element of surprise.

"Do you know Matt's end destination?" Logan asked.

"We need to know how long he'll be on 180 and if he'll be turning on a different road," Em explained.

"Nope. He's headed straight for Silver City. He'll be on 180 for a good while," Herman said.

Perfect. Tom could put out an APB on the rig. And in the meantime, they were close enough that if Logan flew down the road, they could catch them.

"Thank you," Logan said.

"Yes, thank you," Em said as Logan's hand rested on her lower back, ready to head to the Jeep.

"Can I ask..." the woman said.

They paused. "Ask what?" Em replied.

"Who was murdered?" Rita said.

Em looked to Logan.

"My grandpa," he said.

After condolences from Rita and Herman, they were in the Jeep, barreling down 180. Em looked at the speedometer. Seventy miles an hour.

He depressed the gas pedal, and that number rose.

Trees silhouetted by the hazy moon flew by in a blur.

"Call Tom," he said.

"On it." She relayed the information to Tom over Bluetooth while Logan focused his full attention on the road ahead.

"I've got surrounding law enforcement here," he told her. "I'll meet you en route and alert Denton and my fellow officers."

Em disconnected the call, her heart racing with anticipation as the speedometer maxed out at one-hundred and twenty.

The lone road was nearly deserted, and Logan was a superior driver, even at high speeds.

The time couldn't pass fast enough. They had to be on them soon.

"There's a stretch through the pass where it would be easy to cut them off," he said. "If Matt hasn't already passed through and we can get ahead..."

Ahead? "What exactly are you planning?" she asked. Wind rattled the windows.

"You'll see. Just have your gun ready."

She glanced at the floorboard. The gas pedal was flush with it. Her heart pounded, not out of fear but from an odd exhilaration that flooded her whenever they were on a hunt and closing in. They had the drifter—she truly believed they did.

She reached over and clasped her hand over Logan's on the wheel. "We'll get her."

Logan nodded and barreled forward.

Em slid to the side as Tom called back. "Hey, Tom."

"I need your position."

Logan relayed the closest mile marker, not taking his eyes off the road as he wove around a lone car in their lane.

"Be careful," Tom said. "I'll catch up to you in a matter of minutes. I've got backup en route. We don't know if she's armed, and we don't want a hostage situation."

Em gripped the handle over the door, bracing herself as she saw Logan ready to weave again, this time around a semi.

They pulled up on its side, but a logo of apples covered it rather than the XPC symbol.

Sliding into the other lane, they flew by it. Lightning sizzled across the sky, illuminating the truck driver's furrowed face as they pulled beyond him.

The rain that had been threatening to fall started to pour down like a scourge from Heaven. Thick, hard drops pinged off the hood of the Jeep, thumping on the roof, splattering the windshield.

Logan pressed on. The windshield wipers were flying, but the rain fell faster than they could keep up with.

Em blinked, trying to clear her view, but sheets of rain washed down the windshield. The Jeep's headlights illuminated the deluge. Thunder boomed, vibrating in Em's chest, a second after lightning crackled across the black sky.

"There," she said, pointing at another tractor-trailer up ahead.

Logan flew through the pass. When they reached the tractor's side, Em blinked, straining to see anything through the sheets of rain. She rolled down her window, water spurting in, cooling her heated skin. "It's it!" she said. The XPC symbol was barely visible in the rain, but it was there.

"Got 'em," Logan said, pulling past them.

"What are you doing?" She gripped the handle harder. "They aren't going to pull over for us. We need Tom's patrol car," she said.

Determination set Logan's jaw. "Here we go. Hold on."

She did so, her heart fluttering. What was he...? Her body tensed, bracing for the impact she feared would come.

He pulled fifty yards ahead, then slammed the brakes, rocking the Jeep to a stop sideways across the lane. Em jolted forward before she was flung back against the seat.

"You okay?" Logan asked, gun in hand.

She nodded.

"Get out of the car and stand a safe distance away," he said, jumping from the vehicle, his gun in one hand, his badge in the other.

He held both out toward the careening rig as its brakes squealed.

Grabbing a flashlight from the console, she hopped from the Jeep and moved to Logan's side.

"I said get a safe distance," he hollered over the sound-drenching rain.

"I'm by your side, always." She waved her arms, streaking the flashlight across the dark sky.

Please, Lord, let them stop before they reach us.

The rig's horn blared, its brakes screeching as it jackknifed, slinging toward them.

The careening semi's wheels struggling for purchase cast up a flood of water over them.

Em held her breath.

The rig rocked to a stop a matter of inches away.

The driver's side door flew open as Logan raced around to the passenger side.

Em sprinted to cover the back of the rig.

"What in tarnation are you doing?" an unfamiliar man's voice yelled.

"Get off of me," a woman yelled, presumably Mary.

Em edged around the side of the semi in time to see Logan hauling the woman by the waist, her back to his chest as he moved toward the Jeep. She kicked and flailed.

Matt, presumably, rushed forward.

"Special agents," Em yelled out as she darted to the front of the rig to intercept him.

Confusion lit the man's face.

She held up her badge. "Special agents," she repeated. "This woman is wanted for murder."

Matt stopped in his tracks, his eyes widening. "Murder?"

"Yes, sir. Get back in your rig and lock the door, please. Police are en route."

Matt didn't hesitate to do as instructed, and Em rushed to Logan's side.

He had Mary pressed against the Jeep's hood, her hands behind her back. His sketch of her was nearly a perfect replica of the woman.

"Grab me some zip ties from the glove box," he instructed.

Mary struggled against his hold. "You don't know what you're doing! He's coming. He'll get us all."

"Stay still," Logan's commanding voice rang out over the gushing rain.

Grabbing the zip ties, Em hurried back to Logan's side.

"Cover me," he said.

She took position, gun aimed at Mary's head.

He slid his gun in its holster and zip-tied her hands together.

Sirens blared in the near distance. Rapidly flashing red-and-blue lights rounded the bend.

Tom.

He pulled around the rig and came to a fast stop beside them.

Hopping out, he moved for Logan, who was struggling to keep his grip on Mary as she fought his hold.

"He's coming, you fools!" she screamed.

"We've got law enforcement crawling over this entire area, and we have an APB out on his car," Tom announced. "We'll get him."

"He won't go easily," she said, as Tom swapped the zip ties for handcuffs.

"That's okay," Logan said. "He can go any way he likes, but we *will* get him."

Tom shoved Mary in the back of his Tahoe, locking her handcuffs to the silver bar on the back of the front seat. "I'll see you at the station."

"The man?"

"Denton's leading the search. They'll get him." Tom paused, rain lashing off the brim of his Stetson as he slammed the rear door shut. "You can join the search, but I thought you'd want to sit in on her interrogation," he said.

"Absolutely." Logan nodded.

Drenched and shivering, Em rubbed her arms. Logan would get the truth from Mary. He excelled at it. They'd finally know who had pulled the trigger.

THIRTY

Towel dried as much as possible, Logan wrapped yet another dry one around Emmy as water pooled beneath them.

Tom took the first round of interrogation himself, while Logan and Em stood on the other side of the two-way glass. His blood heated, his muscles taut, Logan wanted to go in there and shake the truth out of her. She sat sprawled out, smacking her gum—superficially defiant, yet Logan could see that she was scared. More of the man than of the charges she was facing.

Tom's phone rang, and he stepped out of the room to answer. "Hey, Denton. What's up?" A moment later, he smiled.

Smiled? Logan furrowed his brow, anxious to hear what was going on.

"That's great news," Tom said. "Well done. Okay. We'll see you then. Yes, *we*. Logan and Emmy are here... That's my decision. See you then." He disconnected the call, slipping the phone back into his pocket as Emmy rounded the corner, a printout in her hand. She handed it to Tom, and he studied the information.

"What's up?" Logan asked, aiming the question at both of them. While Tom had been handling the interrogation, Em had been digging into the background of the so-called drifter.

Of course, at this point, Logan knew she wasn't a drifter at all—she was a plant by whoever was orchestrating the Medicare scam. He was betting it was Dr. Keller. The man had no history. And Logan's gut—and, even more importantly, Em's —said it was him. Now they just had to get it out of the woman. It was time to blow this scam wide open before they could graft more money out of the system—or kill another decent, honorable man like Colt.

"Denton got the boyfriend," Tom finally said, clutching the printout by his side.

"Wow. 'Well done' is right." He was impressed. Maybe Denton was a good deputy after all. It didn't mean he had to like him, but he could at least respect his work.

"He's on the way in," Tom said. "Which means we can play them against one another." Tom looked at Logan. "You want to come in and question her?"

"Really?" he asked, eager as a kid. He badly wanted a crack at the woman who'd undoubtedly played a key role in murdering Colt. He'd lay into her hard, showing no mercy as none had been shown to his grandpa.

"The reality is you and Emmy, here," Tom pointed at her behind him, "have been working this case with me since the start. You should help finish it. And officially, your boss arranged for you to have jurisdictional courtesy, so we're on the right side of regulations."

"Thanks, man," he said, clapping Tom on the shoulder.

"But keep it in line. I know it won't be easy." He took off his

Stetson and raked a hand through his hair. "Just restrain your-self in there." He slipped the Stetson back on.

Logan prayed he could. If he went too far, he had no doubt that Tom would throw him out, and he'd lose his chance to get answers.

"Before we go in, you should take a look at this," Tom said, handing him the printout Em had run off the woman's fingerprints.

Logan scanned the page. "Mary Ann Bellum. Age twenty-three." Young for a murderess—if she'd been the one. "Arrested for drug possession twice..." His eyes skimmed the page for the pertinent information. "And shoplifting?" He looked up and frowned. "That's it?"

"That's it," Em answered.

"It's a far cry from murder," Logan said. Not at all what he expected. "How do you go from shoplifting to running a major scam?" he asked.

"Someone recruits you and teaches you," Em said.

"Keller," he said. The expressions on Tom's and Emmy's faces said they were all thinking the same thing.

"We need to get that out of her," Logan said.

"And we will," Tom said, looking back at the glass.

The woman shifted in her seat, stretching her gum out and twirling it around her finger.

Lovely.

"Speaking of gum," Em said, "this came in over the fax while I was running her priors." She handed Tom the other paper.

He scanned it and smiled again.

"What is it?" Logan asked.

Tom looked to Emmy and gave a nod.

"The DNA on the gum found in Colt's stolen truck

matches the woman sitting in that chair," Em said, tilting her chin towards the glass.

Logan closed his eyes on a disappointed sigh. He'd been hoping the gum would turn out to be tied to the man. With the woman, she could claim the gum dated back to the times Colt had lent her his truck. But the man had no legit reason for his DNA to be there. Still, the woman could give them all the evidence that they needed, if Logan could convince her to talk. They needed a confession ASAP.

"You ready?" Tom asked.

Logan nodded, then looked at Em. Her gaze said it all. He had this, and she'd be waiting right on the other side of the two-way glass.

Please be with me, Father. Help us get the truth from her so that she and the others can face justice for what they've done.

After a deep inhale and exhale, he followed Tom into the interrogation room.

The woman was slumped in the chair, her legs splayed out in front of her, smacking her gum.

Tom sat, and Logan took the chair beside him.

"Who are you?" she asked, jutting out her chin.

He realized that he hadn't given his name when he'd taken her into custody. Just his rank as a special agent.

"This here is Special Agent Logan Perry," Tom said.

Her bloodshot eyes glanced to him. "So you're one of the special agents." Disdain dripped in her voice.

"I'm also Colt Tucker's grandson. You killed my grandpa," he said, straight to the point.

She straightened and wrapped her arms across her midsection. "I didn't kill nobody."

"The evidence would suggest otherwise," Tom said.

"What evidence?"

Logan wanted to knock the cockiness from her voice. Instead, he balled his hands into fists beneath the table, releasing and compressing them over and over, trying to distract himself from the driving urge to lunge across the table and wrest the truth out of her.

"The facts are," Tom began, "you stayed on his property, and more importantly, you were the last person seen on the ranch before Colt's murder. An eyewitness can place you there within an hour of his death."

Logan took a steeling breath. Bucky would swear to her presence under oath.

"So I was there. So what? That don't prove nothing," she said, kicking her leg forward, the rubber bottom of her tennis shoe squeaking against the tile floor.

"Your DNA was found in Colt's stolen truck," Tom continued.

She shrugged a flippant shoulder. "I borrowed his truck from time to time."

Tom gave Logan the nod to proceed.

He leaned forward, resting his forearms on the tabletop. "And where did you go in it?"

She shrugged again, her eyes darting down to the floor. "To town to grab stuff."

"Really?" Logan said, scooting forward. "That's interesting, because no one remembers ever seeing you in town, let alone buying anything."

"Maybe people forgot. What's the big deal?"

"The big deal is my grandpa is dead, and you either murdered him in cold blood or you sat by while your boyfriend did."

She blinked rapidly. "My boyfriend? I don't got a boyfriend."

"So the guy you've been running with is...what...your boss?" Logan said, his voice heating.

"I don't got a boss, either."

"Really." Logan sat back and hid a smile. He had her. She just didn't know it yet. "So Keller's not your boss?" he asked, hoping he'd guessed right and hoping even more she'd take the bait.

She swallowed and raked a hand through her tangled hair. "I don't know who that is."

"We both know you're lying," Logan said with confidence. Her blanched face said it all. "Look, you can go down for murder and let your guy friend and Keller get away with everything they did, or you can tell us the truth."

She leaned forward at the waist, her arms wrapping tighter about herself. "You don't know what you're talking about," she muttered.

Em opened the door as planned. "I've got that information you wanted," she said, leaving the door wide as Denton passed by with the man.

Red flared in Mary's cheeks.

"You better not have said a word," the man hollered at her as Denton paused in front of the door.

Logan bit back a smile. Baiting them was working.

"I heard what you said," she hollered back. "You told him you'd kill me," she said, lunging forward.

This was exactly what they wanted—the two pitted against one another so one would crack.

Logan studied the body language between them, the expressions, the glares. All of his instincts screamed that Mary would be the one to break.

"I'll put him in interrogation room two," Denton said, shoving the man forward.

"I'll run his prints," Em said.

"Don't bother," Mary said. "His name is Jeff Waters."

THIRTY-ONE

"I don't know that chick in there," Jeff grunted. "She's just some crazy drifter I gave a lift to."

"Really?" Tom said, sliding over a picture of him and Mary outside the Grand Sunshine Motel. "I'm guessing you didn't know that the owner has cameras hidden all over the place. Said he gets some unsavory characters." Tom crossed one booted foot over the other. "I imagine you'd fall in that category."

"Whatever, dude. So I shacked up with her for a night. I don't know her."

"That's funny, because she sure seems to know you."

Jeff swiped the corner of his mouth. "I don't know what that crazy lady is telling you, but she was nothing more than a one-night stand."

Tom gave Logan the nod to proceed.

"Oh, she's told us a whole lot," Logan said with a smile, as a knock rapped on the door.

"Come in," Tom said.

Em stepped in. "Here you go," she said, passing him a handful of papers.

"Thank you."

"You're welcome," Em shut the door behind her.

"Well..." Tom thumbed through the pages. "Looks like we've got a long arrest record here." He paused on the last page. "Oh, and this," he said, holding up a rendering of the shoe imprint found at Colt's murder scene. Tom stood, and Logan held his breath.

"Let's just see," Tom said, kneeling by Jeff's right leg.

"What are you doing?" Jeff shifted away.

"I'm going to need to see your foot." Tom laid the rendering on the floor. Logan leaned forward.

Please let it be a match, Lord.

"I ain't putting my foot on that." Jeff scooted further away.

"Why not?"

"I'm not incriminating myself."

Logan smiled. "You just did."

"What are you talking about? Who do you think you are?"

"I'm Special Agent Logan Perry and you killed my grandpa."

"Look, man, I don't know what she's telling you, but I didn't kill nobody."

"Why would she tell us anything if she was just a one-night stand? Or do you tell all your one-night stands that you murdered a man?"

"This is getting out of hand. I didn't murder nobody. She's the one you want."

"The one-night stand chick?" Logan asked, working to keep his voice calm as he stared into the emotionless eyes of his grandpa's killer. This was their guy—he was sure of it. Now they just needed a confession. He had high hopes that they'd soon have Mary's testimony. But that wouldn't be enough. He needed to know for certain Keller—or rather, the man posing as Dr. Mark Keller—was the man who ordered the hit. One of them needed to talk.

An hour after moving back in to work Mary over, she broke.

"Jeff killed him. Not me. I didn't want anything to do with it, but he forced me. Said he'd kill me next if I didn't do as he said."

Logan swallowed hard as she confessed. From the sounds of it, she had been there when Colt was brutally murdered at Jeff's merciless hands.

"And what did he have you do?" Tom asked.

"Make it look like a robbery." Tears slipped down her cheeks in black streaks from her mascara.

"What did you take?" Logan asked, testing her. It had to line up perfectly.

"His gun, a ring..."

"Money?" Logan asked, his throat tightening at the image of them stealing Colt's money out of his pocket as he lay dying.

"Jeff took the money clip."

"From where?" Tom asked, holding out a steadying hand beneath the table, signaling that he'd take it from here...at least until Logan got his raging heartbeat to settle.

"His pants." More mascara-tinged tears streaked down her face, rolling off her chin onto her clutched hand.

"Which pair?" Tom asked. "In one of the drawers? In the closet...?"

"On him," she sobbed. "And he took his watch off him too."

At least she had the decency to sob, but it didn't negate the fact that she'd stood there watching while Jeff stole the money and watch off Colt as he lay dying.

"And you'll testify to all of this?" Tom asked her.

She sniffed. "If you give me a deal."

"I'll note that you cooperated and ask the judge for leniency under the circumstances," Tom said. *Leniency.* Logan squeezed his fisted hands tighter, cutting off circulation, his fingers turning white. The word alone incensed him. Colt was shown no leniency, no mercy...why should she get any? But they needed her eyewitness account. And asking for leniency in her case sat better with him than the idea of giving her immunity in exchange for her testimony. She'd still have to face some consequences for what she did, even if they might not be as harsh as she deserved. And at the end of the day, between her testimony and the matching shoe print they'd finally gotten, Jeff would be behind bars where he belonged.

But there was one more man they needed.

"Who is Keller?" he asked.

"What do you even know about him? I'm betting not much." She sniffed and swiped her nose with the sleeve of her sweatshirt.

"Actually, we know a lot," Logan said, sitting back, "but I want to hear it from you."

She sat quiet, fear fixed in her wide eyes.

"Your leniency depends on your cooperation in *all* aspects of the case," Tom reminded her.

"He'll kill me," she said.

"He can't get you in here," Tom assured her.

"Maybe not, but he'll find a way if I turn on him."

"Not if he's in jail, too," Logan said.

"You don't know him." She shifted. "I didn't even know how bad it was until Jeff told me."

"Told you what?"

"That Keller whacked the man Jeff replaced."

"Keller killed a man, personally?"

She nodded, then swiped at her nose again. "That's what Jeff said, and I believe him. Keller's cold-blooded. He creeps me out."

Tom stood. "I'll be right back."

"What's his real name?" Logan continued, knowing that Tom was calling Albuquerque PD to arrest Keller for murder.

Mary narrowed her eyes. "How do you know—"

"Don't worry about that. Just tell me his real name."

She shifted.

"Come on, Mary. There's no leniency unless you cooperate. I need to be able to tell the judge that you shared everything you know," Logan said, nudging harder.

"I only saw his name once, on a passport I found in the nightstand drawer at his lake house."

"Lake house?" Logan straightened.

"Yeah." She shrugged. "Out east somewhere. A...Ash...no Aspen—"

Logan leaned forward. "Aspen Lake?" The latitude and longitude Colt had noted down. It was all coming together.

"That's it," she said, leaning forward. Something shifted in her gaze, in her body language. She wanted this guy behind bars as badly as they did, just for different reasons. She rubbed her arm. "He took me there once. Said I could use the lake house as a retreat." She let out a bitter laugh. "I was dumb enough to believe I'd be safe there." She looked down.

"He raped you," Logan said, needing it spelled out for the record.

Mary nodded, her gaze still downcast. "Yes," her voice was softer than he'd heard it before.

"He'll go to prison for that, too," he said, and she looked up.

How had she gotten tangled in this mess in the first place? Part of him wanted to ask, but that was not where his focus needed to be right now. Besides, even though he felt some pity for her, it didn't negate the fact she'd stood by and watched Jeff kill Colt. His grandpa had shown her kindness and in return... "Why were you staying on Colt's ranch?" he asked.

"Keller said your grandpa was getting wise to the scam. He'd even called Keller's unit at the hospital asking questions. He said he'd staked out Colt for a while, saw that he helped people out and had bunkhouses. He sent me in to pose as a drifter looking for a place to stay."

Logan pumped his fists, blood gushing red-hot through his fingers. "And my grandpa gave you a place out of the kindness of his heart," he managed to say through clenched teeth, his jaw grinding.

She nodded, more tears slipping free.

"Then what?" he asked.

"When he...Colt...your grandpa got too close...Keller sent Jeff in."

"To kill Colt?" Logan asked, needing it on the record.

"Yes."

Silence hung thick in the ten-by-ten room.

Logan looked back at the glass, knowing Em was on the other side. The runaway racing of his heart stilled just knowing she was there.

"He's got the watch, by the way," she said.

"Who? Keller?"

"Yes. Jeff told him what we took, and he wanted the watch. So, Jeff shipped it off to him and popped the money clip in too."

"And Colt's gun?" he asked.

"At a pawn shop by the Grand Sunshine Motel." She shrugged.

Logan exhaled the anger rushing through him. He'd contact the pawn shop as soon as it opened in the morning. For now, he needed to remain calm and focused. "Let's get back to the name on the passport you saw at Keller's lake house," he said.

"You sure he won't get me?" she asked.

"You're safe with us." It felt wrong to say after what she'd done, but it was the truth. She'd go to jail as she deserved, but they weren't going to allow Keller to harm her.

"It's Samuel Wellington III," she answered.

"Samuel Wellington. Thank you." He stood and moved for the door.

She lurched forward. "Where are you going?"

"To give Tom the information."

"Don't leave me in here."

Tom entered before Logan could exit.

"We got his name—it's Samuel Wellington III," Logan said, "I was just about to go give it to you. Did Albuquerque PD bring him in?"

"Let's talk in the hall," Tom said.

Mary stood, pushing the chair back. "I knew it. He's out there, and he's coming for me."

"Mary, you're safe here. We aren't leaving you," Logan assured her. Man, this guy really had her spooked. "We're just stepping into the hall."

"Don't bother. I already know what the sheriff's going to say." She lifted her chin at Tom. "Keller's in the wind."

Logan looked at Tom, and he nodded.

"We've alerted the border agents, and the Albuquerque PD has set up checkpoints leading out of the city," Tom said.

"How'd he even know to run?" Mary asked. "Last he heard, Jeff was going to kill me."

"Your arrest made the news before we even hit the station."

Perspiration beaded on her forehead as she paced the small

room. Back and forth. Back and forth. "We've been here for hours. Who knows where he is by now."

Logan looked at his watch. She was right, but it still wasn't enough time for him to cross the border into Mexico. "Where else might he go?" he asked Mary.

She just kept pacing.

"Mary," he said again. "Don't you want him behind bars? Help us out."

She stopped moving. "His lake house," she said, biting her lip.

"We know the general location of the lake, but we need an address," Logan said. He'd forgotten to tell Tom about the coordinates in all that had been going on, but they still needed an address. There were too many houses surrounding the lake.

"I don't know the address." Mary shook her head. "I just know it's by the lake."

"Do you remember what the house looks like?"

She nodded. "But you aren't taking me there to find it. I'm not leaving this station until he's caught."

Tom opened the door wider and called for Em.

"Yes?" she said, entering, her loving gaze holding Logan's for a brief moment before fixing on Tom.

"Keller owns a house up at Aspen Lake. Can you track it down for us?"

"I can," she said, "but it's going to take a different approach."

Tom narrowed his eyes. "What do you mean?"

"The only residence registered to Dr. Mark Keller is his home in Albuquerque."

"Try Samuel Wellington III," Tom said.

"No, that won't be it," Logan said, thinking out loud. "He wouldn't use his real name for a place he didn't want to be found." His thoughts raced, pinging between all the facts they knew—all the hunches. "Try Dr. Kenneth Sighn"

Tom's brows furrowed. "Oh, the doc on the Medicare claims?"

Logan nodded and prayed his hunch would pay off.

Fifteen minutes later, Em returned with a smile. "Got 'im."

THIRTY-TWO

A drenaline burned Logan's limbs. He lay in the forest ground cover beside Em, staring through a pair of binoculars at Keller's...or rather, Wellington's lake house.

He wasn't home when they arrived.

Logan swallowed, praying they'd played the right card and that he just wasn't at the house yet.

Tom held position on the south side of the cabin. Denton on the east. He and Em were on the north. The west bordered the lake, which was a clear shot for Denton and them.

"He'll come," Em whispered.

"How can you be so sure?"

"Because I have faith. I can feel it. He'll show."

Twenty minutes later, he was clinging to that faith when a black Jeep Cherokee drove down the road.

Logan held his breath to see if it would bear right to Keller's cabin or left to the cabin around the lake.

He veered right, and Logan lifted a silent prayer of praise, but their work wasn't over. They still had to catch him.

"We'll move in once he's in the house," Tom said over Logan's earpiece. "We move too soon, and we risk him fleeing."

The mere minutes it took Keller to collect his grocery bags and step to the front door seemed to Logan to take hours.

Reaching the door, Keller turned, surveying the land.

They held still as his gaze flashed over the ground by their position.

He turned back to the door, and Logan had started to breathe a sigh of relief when Keller dropped the bags and raced for his vehicle.

"He's running," Logan hollered.

"Move in," Tom rapidly replied over the earpiece.

Logan broke into a run, Em by his side. They streaked across the grass as Keller made it to his car.

They were going to be too late.

He aimed his gun. "I need to fire at his tires," he said over the earpiece, knowing he needed Tom's permission even as his gut screamed to just do it.

"I'm clear," Tom said. "Coming around the west side of the cabin."

"Denton?"

"Clear," he replied, and Logan fired.

Whoosh. The bullet flew, missing Keller's rear tire by an inch. He only had one more chance before Keller rounded the bend at the lake's edge and it became a car chase. He inhaled, holding it, then squeezed the trigger. Four rounds in a row, each hitting its mark.

Keller swerved, his Jeep ramming into the towering brick mailbox. His car door opened, and he exited, a sidearm in hand, waving it across the open space, looking for his mark.

"Gun!" Logan yelled as a bullet flew past him, colliding with the tree beside him.

"Take the shot!" Tom hollered.

Logan fired, nailing Keller in the shoulder.

Keller lifted his wavering arm, firing again, this time hitting the ground.

Logan fired again, nailing Keller in the knee.

Keller wobbled, flailing over until he landed on the ground, the gun jarring from his hold.

"Moving in," Tom said over the earpiece.

"In, too," Denton said.

"Covering." Logan held position, ready to fire again if necessary. Emmy too.

Within less than a minute, both Tom and Denton descended on Keller.

Tom retrieved Keller's gun as the doc cussed up a storm while writhing about.

Denton moved in, rolled him over and handcuffed him as Tom covered.

"We're clear," Tom said. "Situation contained."

The air brisk in his lungs, Logan raced forward, Em close on his heels.

They reached the others in time to watch Denton haul Keller to his feet—blood soaking his sweater and pant leg.

Logan looked at Tom, and he nodded. No words needed between longtime friends.

With a smile, Logan walked up to Keller.

Keller looked at him like he was a piece of trash. "Am I supposed to care who you are?"

He decked Keller, knocking him off his feet.

Logan bent over him. "I'm Colt Tucker's grandson."

THIRTY-THREE
ONE WEEK LATER

Logan stood at the foot of Colt's grave on the ranch next to Mee-Maw's. The sinking sun cast rays of gold across the fresh earthen grave—a simple white cross at the top of it.

Beloved husband and grandfather.

But most of all, a cowboy.

Logan smiled at the epitaph. Colt would have liked it.

Em's arm wrapped around his shoulder, pulling his thoughts to her.

How long had he been standing there? The memorial service had been short, as Colt would have wanted it, but still moving. Nearly the entire town of Cauldron Creek had shown up, along with every one of Colt's close family members.

Colt wouldn't have wanted all the fuss, but Logan wasn't turning anyone away.

The horses neighed in the distance. They seemed to know.

"I brought you coffee," Em said, passing him the mug. "You're cold." She cupped her hands over his freshly calloused ones. It'd only been a week since they'd wrapped up the case, but they'd spent it riding every day, his hands getting used to the life of a cowboy again.

"I'm warm now," he said at her touch.

"The gang made dinner," she said, gesturing back in the direction of the house. "No rush, but I wanted you to know."

Five of his seven teammates had come for the funeral, the other two holding down the fort—the rest on call. They'd leave tomorrow, and he and Em would be due back at work on Monday.

He cast his gaze up. The mountains were rugged and beautiful. He looked up at the gray-blue sky of coming twilight that seemed to go on for miles. This was home.

He looked at Em, feeling warm just at the sight of her smile. *She* was his home.

"What are you thinking?" she asked, rubbing his arm.

"You're breathtaking." She was. The last streaks of sun lit her gorgeous brown hair as it tumbled across her shoulders.

She smiled and dipped her chin down.

Holding the coffee in one hand, he tipped her chin back up with the other. "I mean it. You. Are. Breathtaking." He pressed a kiss to her lips. "I only wish he could have met you. He would have loved you."

He took her hand in his.

"And I would have loved him."

With one last glance at the cross, he turned back for the house, Em at his side.

After an hour and an amazing meal of Carolina BBQ, baked beans, and coleslaw, Noah asked if he'd join him for a walk.

"Sure," Logan said, grabbing his coat off the hook. The temps were dropping, the cold of a desert night creeping in. Coyotes howled in the distance as they stepped outside. "Walk or short hike up one of the trails?" he asked his boss.

"Either is fine. As long as the coyotes don't eat us." Noah laughed.

"Considering we're both packing, I wager they'll leave us alone."

"Then let's take a trail."

Logan led the way up the closest trail, heading up the west side of the sloping mountain. Soon, they were in the thick of the trees.

"It's beautiful here," Noah said.

"Yeah. It is."

"Different from anything I've ever seen," Noah added.

"Yeah," Logan tipped his cowboy hat. "I suppose it is."

Noah looked over at him. "You miss it here."

"I do. I didn't realize how much until I was back here for more than a few days." He glanced over his shoulder at Noah. "Thanks for so much time off for both me and Em."

"No need to thank me."

Of course his boss wouldn't ask for thanks. That was just who Noah was.

"You okay coming back Monday?" he asked, taking long strides behind him up the now inverted trail. "You need more time?"

"No. I'm good, thanks."

"But you're not coming back for good." Noah let the statement hang there.

"That depends," he said.

"On Em?"

Logan nodded.

"You know I'll respect whatever decision you both make, but I'll sure be sad if I'm going to be losing two gifted agents... and friends," he added.

He glanced back at his boss. "Thanks, man."

"We've got your back no matter where you are."

E m smoothed her Wranglers, having taken a liking to the western jeans. The boots fit well, as did the black, felt cowboy hat Logan had driven her all the way to The Man's Hat Shop in Albuquerque for. Wilmington seemed a world away. Somehow, this land, so foreign to her when she arrived, now felt like home. It was odd how it had seeped into her blood in her time here with Logan. She didn't want to lose their alone time together—the horseback rides exploring the vast ranch, watching the sunrise from the front porch with coffee. It was all so memorable, like it lived in her skin—so fresh and alive inside her.

"Knock, knock," Logan said behind her. She turned to find him in the doorway, leaning against the frame. His blue eyes met hers under the brim of his Stetson.

"You and Noah have a good walk?" she asked.

"Yeah. We did. Can we go for one?" he asked.

"Sure."

"Grab your new jacket. It's getting chilly out." She did so, and they excused themselves from the team before heading out the back door, this time to the long trail that weaved through the east pasture.

He rubbed the back of his neck. "You ready to go back on Monday?" An edge of sadness clung to his deep voice.

"Are you?" she asked.

He inhaled, then released it slowly. "Em," he said, taking her hand. He tugged her toward him as he backed against a fence post, then tugged her closer still.

"Logan..." She released a whispered giggle. They'd remained as platonic as possible with the team there, but with all their teammates being talented investigators, there'd really been no point. They could easily "read the room," as the saying went.

He brushed her long hair behind her shoulder, then ran his hand along the brim of her hat. "I'll miss seeing you in this." A bittersweet smile hovered on his lips, his eyes creasing at the corners.

"I'll miss the boots," she said, extending her leg. "They are so comfy."

He chuckled, then his face turned serious as his fingers intertwined with hers. "I'll miss being here with you."

She bit her bottom lip. "Me, too."

He leaned in, pressing a kiss to the tender spot at the base of her ear, then lifted his lips to hover over her skin, the warmth of his breath tickling her neck. "What if we stayed?"

A thrill shot through her. "You mean longer?"

He tightened his hold on her hands. "I mean permanently."

She blinked.

He pulled back and dropped to one knee. "I know this isn't the perfect proposal..." He pulled Mee-Maw's ring from his jean pocket. "But..."

She smiled at the sight of his grandmother's ring, then cast her gaze to his—the depth of love shining in his eyes staggered her.

"I don't know where to start...I tried practicing in the mirror, but..." He chuckled and looked down. After a moment's hesitation, he looked back up. His gaze was fierce, brimming with emotion and steadfastness. "I've loved you for so long. But, before...back then, I knew I didn't deserve you."

She dropped to her knees and cupped his face.

He chuckled. "I'm the one that's supposed to be on my knee, remember?"

"I remember the first day I saw you." She caressed his

cheek. "I felt something that day I can't describe, but it burrowed in my heart and has only grown stronger."

He cupped his hand over hers. "Be my wife, Em?" He nudged her nose with his. "Be my wife," he whispered.

Warm tears tumbled down her cheeks and she pressed her lips fully to his.

He smiled against her lips. "Is that a yes?"

"Most definitely a yes."

He wrapped his arms around her and deepened the kiss. The first of what he prayed would be a lifetime full.

EPILOGUE

Nine months later, Em strode out of the house with her cell phone in hand to find her husband on the porch swing. Nausea sloshed in her gut as she held out the phone. Today was the day. "Tom's on the line," she said.

"Hey, Tom," Logan said, switching it to speaker so she could hear. "What's the word?"

"The verdict should come any minute. I'm heading back in the courtroom now, but I'll text you as the verdict is read."

"Thanks, Tom."

Logan sat forward, and Em took the seat beside him as they awaited the last verdict. They'd been at the trials every day except the past three. She'd been sick as a dog, and Logan had insisted on staying home with her. Tom would let them know the verdict in Jeff Waters' case, but she wished her husband could be there to hear it read.

So far, Mary Ann Bellum had been convicted for serving as an accomplice to first-degree murder, hindering a murder investigation, evading the law, and a handful of smaller charges. She'd serve well-deserved time. Samuel Wellington III would be rotting in jail for a very long time for his crimes. In an attempt to gain leniency, Jeff Waters had testified against his former boss, stating that Samuel Wellington III aka Dr. Mark Keller aka Dr. Kenneth Sighn had killed the man he replaced, Layton Parks. He had directed the police to where he'd helped bury the body. Forensic evidence had done the rest.

Em's heart pounded as time ticked by, and she reached for Logan's free hand.

He took it, and she rubbed her index finger along his koa-wood-and-tungsten wedding band.

His knee bounced, and hers twitched in time with it.

The ding of a text sounded. Taking a deep breath, Em looked down.

Guilty of first-degree murder, robbery, evading the law, impeding a police investigation, and aggravated assault. Thankfully, Bobby had survived, or it would have been two counts of murder.

Logan's shoulders softened beside hers, and she rested her head against his chest. "He's going away for a very long time."

Em cupped his face, pressing a kiss to his forehead. Justice had been served. She reached for his hand and smiled at the sight of Colt's watch on his wrist, so thankful they'd retrieved it and Colt's money clip from Keller's lake house. Having them back meant so much to Logan.

"Now," he said, setting his coffee mug down and pulling Em to his side, "as Colt's cipher letter said, it's time to move on. It won't be easy to let go, but it's what he wanted."

The final message to decode had been the cipher, and it had turned out to be a letter Colt had penned to Logan should anything happen to him. It told his grandson that he loved him, was proud of him. Colt had written that should the worst happen, he didn't want Logan to let it eat away at him. That if he was gone, he was with God, riding a horse across the clouds.

Em looked up at the clouds and smiled, wishing she'd met the man this side of Heaven.

Logan caught her gaze and smiled too, the sentiment passing wordlessly between them.

"As soon as you feel better, we'll have to head back up in the clouds," he said of their recent flights in Colt's plane.

"As long as we settle down on all the loops."

"And here I thought you liked those adventures," he said, pulling her close.

"I definitely do, but I probably should start being a little more careful."

Worry creased his brow. "Careful? Is something wrong? I thought you were starting to feel better."

"Nothing's wrong. In fact," she said, pulling the stick from her jean pocket. "It's really right." She handed it to him.

He looked at the pregnancy test, then back at her. "Is that... are we...?"

She nodded, her smile stretching wide. His followed.

"I can't believe it." He pressed a passionate kiss to her lips. When they came up for air, he inched back. "When?"

"Seven months."

"Seven months." His hand rested on her belly. "Seven months." He smiled.

"You up for a new adventure, cowboy?"

"Yes, ma'am." He hovered his lips over hers. "With you, Mrs. Perry, always."

IF YOU ENJOYED THE SHIFTING CURRENT...

Be sure to check out the entire COASTAL GUARDIAN series.

The Killing Tide
The Crushing Depths
The Deadly Shallows
The Shifting Current: A Coastal Guardians Novella

WHAT'S NEXT?

Look for Dani's upcoming Jeopardy Falls series and travel back to New Mexico.
One Wrong Move releases February 2024.

ACKNOWLEDGMENTS

Thank you to all my friends who helped guide me through this new adventure in indie publishing. Susan Sleeman, Christy Barritt, Susie May Warren, Jill Kemerer, and especially Becky Wade for swooping in to save me at the last moment. I deeply appreciate you all.

Thank you to all my faithful friends and readers. I can only share stories because you are there to support me. Joy, Crissy, Amy, Nancy, Renee, Kelly, Debb, Crystal, Stephanne, and all of the Darlings.

I'm so grateful for my family. They lift me up when I'm struggling, put up with "Deadline Mom" and even kick me in the rear and tell me to get back to it when needed. I love you all more than words can say.

Elizabeth and Judy—thank you for all your hard work and keen eyes.

Janet—where would I be without you? Thank you for always having my back, putting up with my rambling emails, and for your sage wisdom and guidance. God blessed me with you.

ABOUT THE AUTHOR

From her early years eagerly reading Agatha Christie and Nancy Drew novels, Dani has always loved mystery and suspense. Now she gets to spend her days combining the page-turning adrenaline of a thriller with the chemistry and happy-ever-after of a romance. Her novels stand out for their "wicked pace, snappy dialogue, and likable characters" (*Publisher's Weekly*), "gripping storyline[s]" (*RT Book Reviews*), and "sizzling undercurrents[s] of romance" (USA Today). Her ALASKAN COURAGE, CHESAPEAKE VALOR, AND COASTAL GUARDIAN series have received praise from readers and critics alike and have appeared on Publishers Weekly, ECPA, and CBA bestseller lists. She researches murder and mayhem from her home in Maryland, where she lives with her husband. When she's not writing, she's hopefully lying on a warm beach, drinking an iced mocha with her nose stuck in a good book.

To learn more about Dani and her books, visit her website at www.danipettrey.com. You can also find her on Facebook as Dani Pettrey and on Instagram as AuthorDaniPettrey. She'd love to hear from you!

Made in the USA
Middletown, DE
02 May 2023

29890594R00125